Anointed Inspirations Publishing

Presents

The Deacon and His First Lady

By:

Tammy T. Cross

ALL RIGHTS RESERVED. No part of this publication may be reproduced, distributed or transmitted in any form or by any means, including photocopying, recording, or other electronic or mechanical methods, without the prior written permission of the publisher, except in the case of brief quotations embodied in critical reviews and certain other noncommercial uses permitted by copyright law. For more information, please contact the publisher.

Copyright © 2018 Tammy Cross

Published by Anointed Inspirations Publishing, LLC

Note: This is a work of fiction. Names, characters, places, and incidents either are products of the author's imagination or are used fictitiously. Any resemblance to actual events or locales or persons, living or dead, is entirely coincidental.

Anointed Inspirations Publishing is currently accepting

Christian Fiction submissions.

For consideration please send manuscripts

to

Anointedinspirationspublishing@gmail.com

Connect with Tammy

Facebook: Author Tammy Cross

Instagram: @Mrsteelady3950

Bentley

After ten years of marriage despite my cheating ways, I can't believe Glinda still finds it in her heart to continue to love me unconditionally. Glinda is a beautiful woman who has no problem finding a good man that would love her how a woman should be loved. I had been the Deacon down at Kingdom Cometh Baptist Church and should have known better than running around on my wife.

Don't get me wrong I love my wife with all my heart but the sight of a beautiful woman makes me weak in the knees. My past relationship with Missionary Gracie Brown a member of the church is the reason we moved from Somerville, Texas to College Station, Texas. We thought it would give us a fresh start with our marriage.

Gracie was a very beautiful woman. Looking at her was like looking into the eyes of Taraji P. Henson. She would come to church every single Sunday with her dresses fitting her body like a glove. She made it a point to sit in the front row every Sunday so that I could get a good peek at her road to glory. Looking at her made me want to do a holy dance. I couldn't focus on the sermon for trying to watch those beautiful thighs of her, but I couldn't stare too long because I had to keep our little affair a secret.

Since our move Glinda and I have been doing well, we have been happier than ever. Our only child Benny who is nine years old seems happier as well. He doesn't have to worry about the kids making fun of him at school because his dad was known for cheating with the Missionary down at the church. Lord knows I hated putting my family in that situation and I've been praying harder than ever to stay on track and make sure I don't hurt my family again.

I got up and got dressed to go down to the church like I did daily. I put on a white button-down shirt with a pair of gray slacks and a pair of black penny loafers. While getting dressed I looked in the mirror on the big cherry wood dresser that was sitting before me. I began to think about what people had to say about me. A lot of them told me that I'm a lucky man to have a lovely wife like Glinda with the way I look. Some even use to tell me, "Bentley you look like Eddie King Jr. from the movie The Five Heartbeats and you shouldn't be running around on any woman." I have a high self-esteem so nobody can tell me I am not handsome. My father taught me at an early age not to let anyone make me feel less than what I am.

I was teased as a kid because of my looks, but I still didn't have a problem getting a pretty girlfriend. They used to tell me I was black, skinny and ugly but even that didn't bother me because I had the girls that they wished they had. So, I just laughed it off and ignored all those harsh names they would call me.

When I was dressed, I walked into the living room where my wife Glinda was sitting watching her favorite movie "Waiting to Exhale". "Honey I am about to go down to the church and help the pastor work on this business deal he's been trying to put together," I told her as I kissed her on the cheek before walking out the door.

"Ok baby you have a good day and tell Pastor Edwards I said hello," Glinda yelled out to me as I exited the side door heading out to the garage to get into my truck and drive down to the church.

Glinda

    Some say that I should have left Bentley years ago when I first found out about him cheating. I didn't leave because I wanted to work things out with him for the sake of our child. Benny had a hard time trying to figure out why the kids at the school were making fun of him and calling him names. After his father's affair, some of the kid's parents were talking about it and their kids overheard them. This is what made them tease Benny and saying some horrible things to him. After months of counseling which didn't help him, we decided to move to give us all a fresh start in our life.

    I do know that I wouldn't have a problem getting a man with me looking like the beautiful Jill Scott the singer. My skin tone is a smooth caramel color and I wore a short shoulder length hairstyle that was like a big curly afro. When I put on an outfit my thick curvy thighs and hips filled it out just right. I wasn't a big woman but I wasn't considered small either. I stood every bit of five-foot-five and yes I'm thick and it's all in the right places.

    When I first found out about my husband's affair with Missionary Gracie I was crushed. She was the only one that I trusted to babysat Benny while I went to work. I never expected her to betray my trust like that. She used to always meet my husband down at the church to work on paperwork for the Pastor or to put together programs. Yes, it's true that sometimes I felt some way about it but then my husband would tell me I was overreacting. I knew I should have followed my gut feeling and dropped in on them from time to time.

The day I got the phone call from Gracie's husband telling me to get down to the church and fast. I was so nerves I thought something had happened to my husband. I grabbed my keys off the key hook by my front door, took Benny to my neighbor to watch in case I had to go to the hospital and drove like a bat from hell to the church. When I pulled in I almost didn't turn the motor off good before jumping out of my little gray Honda Civic.

I must admit I was a little confused at first because I didn't see an ambulance or the police. The way Gracie's husband William sound over the phone I knew it was bad. I felt a knot form up in my stomach when I walked in and called out to William. At first, I didn't see or hear anyone but as I walked farther into the church I heard loud arguing. I had to stop and hold on to the side of one of the pews because I knew what was going on in the pastor's study was not going to turn out well. I ask the Lord to strengthen me as I storm straight to the office like a raging bull.

When I walked into the office I tell you what I saw before me almost made me lose my mind. I knew I had been right all along and this man led me to believe that I was just putting more into his and Gracie's relationship than it really was.

"BENTLEY! What is going on in here? So is this what you do when you come down to the church with this floozy." I looked him in the eyes and yelled out to him.

"Floozy" Gracie snapped back at me as if she was offended.

"Girl don't make me fix those tracks you got glued to the side of your temples that you use to hide your bald edges," Glinda yelled out in anger while holding a tightly closed fist. Gracie couldn't do anything but sit there with her mouth wide open and her hand over the weave that Glinda just called her out on.

"Glinda wait I can explain," Bentley Johnson shouted as he sat on the couch stark naked with his shirt he left the house in wrapped around his behind.

"Gracie, I trusted you. I thought you were my friend. I trusted you and only you to watch my son. I guess this why you didn't let me pay you huh? You were getting your pay by sleeping with my husband." I told her in anger.

"Glinda let me explain baby" Bentley had the nerves to spit out of his mouth right before I twirled my head around like the little girl in the movie "The Exorcist."

Before I could say a word, William stopped me and said, "No Glinda let's see what this chump got to say before I beat him to a pulp."

I looked over at Gracie now in tears and then back at William and realized things in this room have just gotten real. I could tell Bentley had to get his thoughts together before he spoke. He didn't know how he was going to get himself out of this one. Just as he began to speak the pastor came walking in. Bentley sat straight up on the couch and wiped the sweat from his forehead that was pouring down fast as the Jordan River.

"What in God's name is going on in my office? Missionary, Bentley where are your clothes. Wait a minute don't tell me you two were doing the devil's grind right here in the middle of my office." Pastor Edwards yelled out at the two of them.

Neither one of them had a word to say. I moved closer to the pastor to tell him what was going on but he held up his hand and stopped me before I could get one word out.

"Don't y'all just sit there looking crazy now somebody better speak and speak right now. Glinda, I don't need you to explain anything you aren't the one sitting here stark naked." The pastor fussed.

Bentley was holding his shirt tightly around his bottom and tried to stand to his feet. Before he could stand completely up William hit him with a quick two to the body and one right in his eye before the pastor could grab him. Gracie then jumped off the couch and ran to the women's bathroom to get dressed. William was wrestling with the pastor to get loose so he could go after her but the pastor held on for dear life. When he got William calm his man wig had slid off his head.

Before Gracie could exit the room, I grabbed her by the hair and pulled out a hand full of that madden up weave she had in her head. Gracie was so scared I was going to snatch her bald that she ran to the bathroom and locked the door. I didn't want to act up too badly in the church so I turned my focus back on Bentley, the man that betrayed me.

I was so stunned by everything that was going on that I couldn't move another inch. I felt like I wanted to throw up. I looked over at the couch and my husband was laying there holding his now half-closed eye and bleeding mouth. I guess when he hit the floor he hit his mouth on the side of the couch. I needed some fresh air, so I ran out of the church so fast one would have thought someone was chasing me.

When I made it outside I stood up on the side of my car and threw up everything I ate this morning. I unlocked my car and sat down in the seat. My face felt so nasty from throwing up so I reached over and pulled a napkin out of my purse and cleaned my face. Lord knows I was glad I always kept a stash of them in my purse.

After cleaning my face, I laid back in my seat and cried my eyes out. I can't believe I was dumb enough to believe my husband when he said he wasn't cheating. All the signs were there I just ignored them. Man, I feel like the dumbest woman alive. I didn't know what to do next. All I could think about was my son. He would be so devastated if his dad and I separate. I looked up and began to pray.

"Lord you know I have stood by my husband any way I could but what am I to do in a situation like this. Father God you are going to have to help me with this one because I don't know if I can handle this alone. You said you wouldn't put any more on me than I can bear Well Lord, I really need you because I believe this is more than I can bear"

Before I could finish praying I was interrupted by a knock on my car window. I looked up and it was Bentley. He was standing there looking like a deer in headlights. His right eye was almost shut and his lip was so swollen that he looked like he had a fight with a gang of bees. I couldn't stand the sight of him right now so I locked the door and speed off almost running him over.

When I made it home I looked in the rearview mirror to make sure my face was straight before I walked over to my neighbor's house to get Benny. I jumped out the car and made my way to her door and rang the doorbell. I was trying to look as if everything was ok.

"Hey, Glinda is everything alright? How is Bentley?" My neighbor Marsha asked me.

"Yes, girl he is fine. Can you get Benny I really need to get home?' I asked trying not to make eye contact with her.

"Sure, hold on a second," she said as she walked in and led Benny out to me.

I grabbed Benny and began to walk away when Marsha shouted out to me. "Glinda, you know if you need to talk I am here for you."

"Thanks, Marsha I really appreciate that," I shouted right before I turned and went home.

When I made it in the house I sent Benny to his room to hang out. I walked into my room packed Bentley a suitcase of clothes and things for his hygiene and placed them in the garage. I shot him a text message saying. "Hey, I don't think you need to come home for a while. I need time to think and besides Benny don't need to see you like this. You can pick the suitcase up in the garage that I packed for you. Bentley please do what I ask and don't come in because God only knows what I may do."

I was drained from this whole day. I walked into Benny's room and let him know I was about to take a nap and don't open the door for no one I don't care who it is. He agreed and I walked into my room laid on my bed and cried myself to sleep.

Bentley

    Man, I messed up I knew Gracie and I was getting a little too comfortable in what we were doing. Glinda was seeing what was going on so I guess William had a hunch that something wasn't right either. I didn't mean for any of this to happen but Gracie had me under her spell. The way she walks has me hypnotized. The way her hips swayed from side to side will make a blind man turn to peek. I don't know what I would do if I lose Glinda. She has been so good to me and all I did was cause her nothing but pain.

    After leaving the church I drove around for hours trying to clear my head. I thought about Gracie and I wondered if she was ok. Upset as her husband was I pray he didn't go home and hurt her. I then turned my focus on Glinda, what will she tell Benny when I don't come home? Could she ever find it in her heart to forgive me or is this the end of our marriage, was all I kept asking myself?

    I picked up my phone and tried to call and talk things over with her but the call just went straight to voicemail like the other ten times that I called. "Hello, you have reached Glinda I am not able to come to the phone right now but if you would please leave a message, I will get back to you as soon as I can. Thank you and have a blessed day." Was the message I got every time I called.

Once it was dark enough I pulled up to the house and went straight to the garage and grabbed the suitcase of things Glinda prepared for me. I stood in the garage and looked at the door that led into the house and wanted to go in so bad until I thought about the message Glinda had sent me warning me not to try and come inside. I grabbed my suitcase and headed out to the truck threw it in the back seat of my black 2016 Dodge Ram and drove away.

Not knowing what else to do I pulled into Days Inn, Somerville's local motel and got me a room. The motel wasn't too fancy but I was tired and it was a place to lay my head for the night. I felt so horrible for letting Pastor Edwards down. That man has been there for me during the roughest times in my life. When my parents passed I felt like I had died right along with them. Pastor Edwards was there to comfort me and be a listening ear whenever I needed to talk. He is the reason Glinda and I am married now.

I wasn't sure that I was ready to get married but I knew that Glinda was the woman I wanted in my life. One day this lady in town by the name of Debra was trying to get with me and I almost took the bait. Debra was a beautiful woman; she looked so much like Janet Jackson body and all. The only thing about her was she was loose when it came to men. She could be seen with a different man every other week. The older women said that she would change her men like she changes her underwear. When Pastor Edwards got wind of it he sat me down and told me it's time you settle down. Glinda was the woman God had for me. I knew he was right and we were married a few months later.

After sitting on the side of the bed stressing myself out, I got up and walked into the bathroom and took a long hot shower.

The Deacon and His First Lady   *Tammy T. Cross*

The way the hot water was hitting my back felt so good on the bruises I had from the punches William gave me. I tell you if the pastor wouldn't have come in there he probably would have killed the both of us. I looked up and said, "Thank you Lord for Pastor Edwards."

    If someone would walk up to me and tell me this is what happens when you cheat with another man's wife I couldn't say one mumbling word. The way William got my face looking I would mistake myself for Eddie. He really put a number on me. Once I dried off and put my clothes on. I grabbed the cup of ice I got from the lobby and placed it in one of the towels and held it on my eye to try to get rid of some of the swelling.

    As I lay on the bed I pulled my wallet out and looked at the family picture Glinda and I took with Benny around Christmas time last year. It hurt me so bad to look at how happy he was in the picture. He has no clue how messed up I am and yet he loves me so much. I tried to hold back the tears in my eyes to keep them from burning the cuts on my eye but I couldn't fight them back fast enough. I used the towel to try to wipe them away to stop the burning. Even that didn't help but I guess I deserve everything I got.

    The next morning, I woke up and took care of my hygiene. When I looked in the mirror this time my eye was completely closed. Good thing I had a pair of shades in my truck so that when I went out people wouldn't be staring at me. When I was done I picked up the phone and tried to call Glinda once more.

    "Bentley what do you want? You have five minutes to say what you have to say and I am hanging up." Glinda calmly said from the other end of the phone.

"Glinda, I am sorry, I never meant to hurt you, baby. Please forgive me." I begged her.

"Look you should have thought about that before you had me sitting around looking like a fool while you creep around with ole Missionary Gracie," she snapped.

"It was never my intention to hurt you or Benny. I was stupid and begin the deacon of the church I should have known better."

"You're right you should have known better but since you didn't I think its best you stay where you are for a while. I will tell Benny you had to go out of town on some church business." Glinda said before she told me, "Your five minutes is now up. "Then she hung up the phone.

"Glinda, Glin….." I tried to yell out to her, trying to stop her from hanging up.

I can't believe that this is happening to me. I must say I dread making this next call but I know that I must. I picked my phone up off the little twin bed I slept in and strolled through my contacts until I came across Pastor Edwards's number.

After two rings a deep voice answered on the other end of the line saying, "hello there Deacon Ben," that's the name he liked to call me. "I have been expecting a call from you."

"Hey, Pastor I was wondering if there was any chance that I can come down to the church and speak with you?" I nervously asked.

"I was hoping that you would. I really would like to meet with you before William and Missionary Gracie come in to see me. Deacon, can you come now," he asked?

"Sure, Pastor give me ten minutes and I will be there," I told him while grabbing some clothes out of my suitcase to throw on.

Once I was dressed I walk down to the lobby to reserve the room for a few more nights. On my way out, I grabbed a banana nut bread muffin and a cup of coffee from the continental breakfast area and strutted out the door. I got in my truck, said a quick morning prayer and drove over to the church.

When I arrived, I didn't see anybody's car there but the pastor's. I was happy about that because embarrassed as I was I couldn't stand to bump into anyone else down at the church. I jumped out of my truck and walked straight in and right into the pastor's office where he was sitting behind his wooden desk waiting for me.

"Come on in Deacon Ben glad you could make it, just hate the reason that has you here right now." The pastor told me with a stern look on his face.

"I know Pastor and I came because I felt I need to apologize for disrespecting your church."

"Deacon, how long has this mess with you and Missionary been going on. Be straight with me about this man."

"Pastor look…"

"Now don't pastor look anything, Deacon I said to be straight with me man. I don't need a long drawn out story. I want you to answer the question I asked you." He said standing there with the most serious look on his face. Looking just like James Earl Jones the actor from the movie "Coming to America."

"It's been a year Pastor."

"A year deacon, so when were you going to tell me," he yells so loud I thought the church walls were going to cave in.

"Pastor calm down I met Gracie here to end it yesterday but she didn't want it to end. She started to cry and I couldn't stand to see her cry. One thing led to another and William walked in on us and called Glinda."

"Bentley, you let this woman bait you in like that. Let me tell you something, because of the weak actions you have torn apart not one but two great marriages."

All I could do was place my head down on my lap because what he was saying was right. I didn't know if Glinda would ever take me back. If she doesn't I have nobody to blame but myself because my wife is just as much woman as Gracie is. I guess I wanted my cake and eat it too.

"Hold your head up and talk to me. It isn't any use in you thinking now. What were you thinking about when you were rolling around all in Gracie's sugar bowl for a whole year DEACON?...."

"You're right, you are so right pastor maybe I should have been thinking but I wasn't and it is nothing I can do about it to change that now Pastor Edwards. So, what is it that you want me to do." I stood up frustrated and yelled back at the pastor.

"Look boy don't your little skinny behind sass me like that. Do you understand me?"

"Yes Pastor, I am sorry. I didn't mean to yell like that. I'm just so frustrated."

"Good, you should be sorry but to answer your question as to what I want you to do Ben. I need you to step down out of the deacon's position." Pastor Edwards replied.

"You can't be serious after all these years I have devoted to this church and you're asking me to step down. Really Pastor!"

"Yes, really and seems like the only thing you were devoted to was pleasing ole Gracie and up in the church deacon. Man, you better get out of my office with your ugly attitude. Deacon I may be saved but don't give me a reason to have to spend the night at the altar begging God for forgiveness."

I looked into the pastor's eyes and saw that he was playing no games. After all these years I have been serving down at this church I never saw the pastor get this angry before. I didn't want to cause any more trouble so I turned and stormed out of the church.

I made it out to my truck and I unlocked the truck door and jumped in. I sat in the parking lot and banged the steering wheel for a whole minute. I turned and looked back at the church once more before I drove off.

Being a deacon was everything to me and I allowed the devil to come into my life and take it all away from me, within a blink of an eye. All for a little bit of pleasure that I could have easily gotten at home, I feel so dumb.

    I rode out to the lake to clear my head. I am not gonna lie it ran through my mind a few times to jump into the lake and end my life, but the spirit of God wouldn't let me. It appears I could sense that even though I messed up he was still there for me. Then there was Benny who I loved dearly. I couldn't have him thinking I just left him in this cold cruel world alone. I took a deep breath and looked up at the sky and asked God to forgive me for all that I have done.

    When I was on my way back to the motel my phone began to ring it was Glinda. I answered so fast I dang near screamed hello with excitement. "Glinda what's going on?"

    "No, Daddy it's me Benny?"

    "Hey, son how's it going?"

    "I am good Daddy mommy told me you had to go out of town. I miss you when are you coming home?"

    "I'm not sure son, where's mommy?" I asked him trying not to let the hurt in my voice be heard as I spoke with my son.

    "She's right here daddy hold on let me get her. Oh, daddy hurry home and I love you." Benny said sounding so sad.

    I could hear him yelling out to Glinda, "Mommy phone"

    "Hello, who's this?"

    "It's me Glinda Benny called me on your phone. He wants to know when I am coming home."

"Oh my God, I know Benny didn't just do this. He has been asking me to call you and I told him you were very busy. Glinda responded.

"I didn't tell him any different than what you told him. He still thinks I am out of town. Glinda, we can't keep lying to him, it's wrong." I told her.

"Wait a minute I know you aren't talking about lying when you have been lying for a full year." She whispered through the phone letting me know she didn't want Benny to hear her.

"Look I know I was wrong but do we have to talk about this over the phone can you meet me somewhere and we talk about this. I need to know how we can get past this Glinda."

"I don't know if I can deal with this right now Bentley. Let me think about it and when I am ready I will call you until then I will talk to you later." She hung up before I could say another word.

I guess I will be staying another night at the motel is what I said to myself. I ran down to Dairy Queen and ordered me a hunger buster combo and for my drink, I ordered a large coke. I drove a few blocks back to the motel and went in and ate my food. After a day like this, I just wanted it to be over. I didn't have many friends so I just laid down and watched old western shows for the rest of the day.

I must have fallen to sleep because when I woke up it was 7:30 the next morning. I went into the bathroom and washed up for the day. After putting on a light blue polo shirt, a pair of jeans and my retro tennis shoes I sat on the bed to check my phone to see if

Glinda may have called. To my surprise, I had about four text messages from Gracie saying that she had been trying to call me and to please call her back.

The last text message read, "Bentley why aren't you answering my text message. I really need to talk to you. William packed his thing and moved back to his mother's house."

Me being as dumb as I was, I dialed her number and before I could change my mind and hang up she answered. Bentley, why have you been ignoring my phone calls and text messages?

"Gracie look we have to end this. Can't you see we have caused enough problems as it is and you still contacting me?" I told her.

"You can't be serious Ben; I know you love me how can you end this just like that," she cried out to me.

"I have a family I can't keep hurting my wife and my son Gracie. You need to try and work this out with your husband because what you and I had is over." I told her as I hung up the phone because I couldn't stand to hear her cry any longer.

Gracie called my phone back to back so I turned it off to avoid her calls. After an hour I powered it back on and deleted all her voicemails without listening to them completely. Right before I deleted the last message I heard that it was Glinda which said, Bentley, I am going to give you a chance to talk. Meet me at Nana's restaurant downtown at 11:00 a.m. I looked over at the clock I still had a little time so I sat at the table in the corner and had a little talk with God. I had been so wrapped up with Gracie until I think I forgot who God really was until on Sundays. Which I barely did there too because I was too busy peeking at Gracie.

I sat in my chair and spoke to God from my heart. "God, I know that for this past year I have been living in sin and I am not too proud of myself right now. I have torn up my family and now I am lying to my son. Lord, I sat here today to confess all my sins to you and ask you for forgiveness. I don't know if I could make it without Glinda and Benny. The two of them are my world. Lord, I am going to meet Glinda today and I ask you to work this out for us. Lord if you give me another chance I will do better. Lord, I am putting this situation in your hands and I am trusting and believing that you already have this handled. Amen.

I sat at the table in silent thinking about what I would say to her. Before I knew it, it was time for me to go. I got up to put on a splash of Joop her favorite cologne and strutted out the door. I jumped in my truck took one last look in the mirror. My eye was still looking swollen so I threw on my shades and drove over to the restaurant.

When I arrived, Glinda was already inside waiting. I jumped out my truck and walked inside. I really have to admit she was looking good. Her hair was whipped to perfection; her make-up was applied so beautifully. She had on a purple sundress with a pair of silver sandals. That made her purple and silver eyeshadow she has on look lovely as ever. She looked like an angel sent straight from heaven. I stared at her the whole walk to the table.

"Bentley, I am glad you could make it on such short notice." She said to me with a slight smile that could light up the world.

"Glinda when I got your message I knew I had to come. I owe this to you. Nobody did this to us but me, so I knew I had to be here." I responded rambling on trying to find the right words to say.

"That you are right about. Before we get started I should let you know I took it upon myself to order the both of us a fish plate. It comes with fish, fries, and coleslaw, which I know is your favorite." She informed me.

"Thanks, Glinda," I responded as I picked up the glass of water that she also took upon herself to have them bring out for me.

"I know nothing I say can change the fact that I cheated on you, but I am asking you to forgive me. I never meant to hurt you."

"SOOO how did you think I was going to feel. After all, the man I vowed to God to spend the rest of my life with was caught sleeping with the missionary at our church." Glinda told me with hurt in her voice.

"I understand where you are coming from and I know I don't deserve a woman like you but I am asking you to give me another chance to prove my love for you and Benny."

"Oh no, you don't Bentley don't go dragging Benny in this. This is about you and me only right now," she fussed.

"I respect that Glinda, but I am asking you to let me come home," I begged her.

She sat there as if she was thinking for a moment and after her not saying anything I knew she was lost for words to say.

"I do want to be completely honest with you. Gracie has been reaching out to me I talked to her once and told her it was over. I also told her that I had a family that I want to make things right with." I said to Glinda scared she would get up and walk out but I had to be honest.

"Oh, yea and what did she have to say about that." She asked patiently waiting for an answer.

"She told me that William packed up and left and basically thought that she and I still had a chance but I had to let her know there wasn't and hung up when she began to cry."

"I can't believe she had the nerve to cry over someone else husband. Really tell me where they do that at?" Glinda said.

Our food finally arrived we ate in silence and I didn't care about the silence as long as I was in the presence of my beautiful wife.

Once our food was done she finally told me, "Bentley I am going to give you a chance to come home but if this happens again you will lose Benny and I. Oh and one more thing I want to start over and move to College Station, Texas since that's where my new job will be."

"That's fine babe just as long as I am with you and Benny." I said wanting to jump up and hug her but not knowing how she would react."

She then reached over the table and pulled the shades off my eyes to look at the damage that Williams caused me for sleeping with his wife." Oh my God, your eye looks terrible. On your way back to the motel stop by Family Dollar and grab you a bottle of witch hazel to clean up the bruising and I will tell Benny you are on your way home and you got hit in the eye by a doorknob."

I jumped up and gave her a hug. I then paid the ticket and we went our separate ways. I drove over to Family Dollar grabbed some witch hazel and cotton balls and checked out. When I got back over to the motel I hurried up and loaded my belonging into my truck and then checked out of the motel. I then headed home to my family saying to myself, "Thank you, Jesus."

Gracie

Pastor Edwards wants William and me to come to the church today and sit down and talk with him. I don't know how I am going to convince him into going. William hasn't said a word to me since we left the church. He has been sleeping in the guest room and eating dinner at his mother's house. Since he decided to move back home. This was as good as she wanted because she couldn't stand the ground that I walked on. I hated I messed up but Bentley treated me like a woman should be treated while William had been ignoring me.

I tried to warn him and tell him that I need his attention and he would always say he was tired from working so hard. I mean we never did anything together like we used to. We never even go places; it was as if I didn't even exist to him. I guess that's why when I started getting the attention I needed from Bentley it was so easy for me to cheat on William. I am far from happy with what happened between us but it did; now it's over so he should just suck it up and let it go.

Now he wants to sit around and act as if I caused all of this and he didn't play a part in this. I looked at the clock and it was almost time to go meet the pastor. William was lying on the couch looking like a sick puppy.

I walked into the room and asked him, "William did Pastor Edwards call you?"

"Yes, he did and I told him there was no need for me to come I wasn't the one who was caught with my clothes off." He said with anger all in his tone.

"Look, William, this is something that happened and it's over with so why are you still holding all of this anger in." I spit at him before walking away.

"Gracie, you got some nerves making this out to be my fault. I didn't cheat you did." He jumped up walking behind me yelling.

I turned around and looked him in his face and cried, "Well if you would have listened to me when I told you I needed you and how lonely I was this wouldn't have happened. I cried out to you for affection over and over and you just let it go in one ear and come out the other. So yes, William this is your fault."

He stood there looking like a plum fool. I guess the cat had his tongue because he sure didn't have anything to say. I could have just slapped him silly but he was looking too good to me. This man weighed about 180 pounds. He had a light brown skin color and looked just like David Harrington from "The Haves and Have Not." When he noticed how I was staring at him he stormed off to the room and threw on a pair black polo jogger and a black and white t-shirt to match it. He sat on the side of the bed and slid on a pair of Nike socks and his black and white forces. He then grabbed his keys and walked out the door yelling I will meet you at the church.

I ran behind yelling, "are you really going to leave without me, William. What will Pastor Edwards think about that William?"

"The same thing he thought about catching you on his couch but did you care about that?"

I guess he gave me a taste of my own medicine because when he said that I couldn't say a mumbling word. I turned and walked back into the house. I grabbed my coach purse off my dresser and searched through it for my key. I walked out of the house locking the door behind me. I ran out to my car, got in and drove over to the church.

When I arrived, William had already gone inside. I parked my car in my favorite parking spot right in the front of the church. I got out and walked in and went to Pastor Edwards's office. He and William were already engaged in a conversation, so I just waved hello to the pastor and took and sat in the empty chair next to William.

"Hello Missionary Gracie, how are you this fine day?" Pastor Edwards asked me.

"I am fine and you Pastor," I replied in a dry tone.

"I couldn't be better Missionary. Now let's get to the reason you are here today." Pastor Edwards said with such a serious tone in his voice.

I swallowed hard and was ready to answer any question he had for me.

"I have talked to Bentley and I have asked him to step down from Deacon of this church," he informed me.

"You did what Pastor? How could you do that and this man has spent years serving and doing good deeds for this church? He was here when you couldn't be and you want to dismiss him." Gracie blurted out in anger.

He'd had enough. Pastor Edwards stood up and yelled out, "How dare you to come in here and act like you two didn't do anything wrong, and you did it in my office. And only God knows how many times Gracie."

When he called me by my government name like he did I knew he was upset. I sat back and didn't say another word.

"Now, I am going to give you a chance to tell me your side of the story. You can start by telling me just how long this mess been going on with you and Bentley." The pastor sat back down and asks me in a voice so calm it made me think he was having a bipolar moment. One minute he was yelling the next he was calm as a cool breeze.

"I paused a minute before I spoke. I then looked the pastor straight in the eye and he gave me a look to let me know he wanted nothing but the truth. I glanced over at William and said, "We have been messing around for a year now."

William jumped up and shouted, "What!!! A whole year Gracie??? When were you going to tell me?"

"Calm down William let's see what else she has to say for herself, Gracie was it here in my office?" asked the pastor.

"Sometimes it was but most of the time I would park my car here and he would pick me up and we would ride over to Caldwell to the motel there since this town was so small. We knew no one would notice Bentley's truck and call Glinda. I told them since they just had to know everything.

"Gracie, you are a disgrace to this church. You are strutting up in here Sunday after Sunday acting like you are sanctified and all that and the biggest whoremonger in this church. Gracie, you can no longer serve on any committee any kind of way at this church." Pastor Edwards made clear to me.

"Pastor, you can't do that I been here for years and I made sure all of your programs were planned out nicely and made sure everything here was in order," I shouted out to him.

"Gracie, I agree with the pastor. You can't be coming up in here acting any kind of way and expect things to keep running like they are. Who wants a missionary that sleeps around at the church in the pastor's office at that?" William spoke out and said.

"You would take his side, William. You can't stand the fact that another man was giving me the attention I was begging you for can you." I said before I got up and stormed out of the church.

I left the Pastor and him sitting in the office looking like two crash dummies. I got in my little blue Kia and speed off. When I made it home William was storming through the door right behind me. Still trying to talk to me but I just walked into our bedroom and ignored him. I was done talking.

"Well since you don't have anything more to say I do. I am packing my things and moving out and this time I am not coming back." He said as he grabbed a suitcase and filled it up with his belongings. He came back in the house and packed out some more of his things about three times, before he walked out saying, "I will be back later for the rest of my things."

I know I was trying to be hard and all but with him packing his clothes out like he was I knew he meant business this time. I ran to the door trying to beg him not to leave but he just ignored me and jumped in his car and drove off. He was so angry I prayed that he didn't hurt himself or anyone else as fast as he was driving away.

I walked back into the house and sat down on the couch thinking what a mess I have caused. I broke up my marriage and now I am all alone. I didn't think it was fair because Bentley had just as much to do with this as I did and he still has his family. I thought to myself "I am going to give him some time and he will be calling my phone I just know it he can't stay away from me.

Hours had passed by and I haven't heard from my husband I think it is really sinking in that I have really lost him. I know he really loved me but I needed more and Bentley did that for me. Now I am sitting here thinking maybe I just thought I needed more. Either way, it goes there is no need in sitting here trying to worry about a thing now. It's over and there is nothing else that can be done about it.

I walked around the house and started taking down all the photos that we had taken as a couple and placed them out in a box in the garage. I then walked back to my room and sat on the side of my bed staring at the wall. After a while, I laid back on the bed and felt something hard hit the side of my arm. When I looked over I was crushed at what I saw. Tears began to fill my eyes and all at once I started crying uncontrollably. If I didn't want to believe what was going on I had no other choice but to believe it now.

I cried for a couple of hours before I pulled myself together. Once I was done I reached down to the bed and picked up the wedding ring that my husband once faithfully wore. The only way he would take it off was to clean it and it went right back on. William told me that when he said his vows he meant every word he said and he did just that but I guess even a good man knows when enough is enough.

Days went by and weeks turned into a couple of months and I still hadn't heard a word from William nor Bentley. At this moment I didn't care anymore about William but Bentley got some nerves ignoring me. I didn't put a gun to his head to make him sleep with me. I quit smoking years ago but today I needed one bad as ever. I jumped in my car rode down to the corner store and bought a pack of Newport shorts in the box and a lighter. Before I could get out the store good I had already popped one in my mouth and lit it up. Man, the menthol sure did taste good in my mouth. I tilted my head back and blew the smoke out my mouth real slow. I then returned to my car and drove in the direction of Bentley's house hoping to see him outside.

When I pulled on the street I felt like someone had stabbed me in my chest with a steak knife. "I know this can't be happing right now." I said to myself as I stopped my car directly in the front of the house."

I sit there looking like a total fool. "I can't believe Bentley would do this to me." I parked the car and got out to take a closer look to make sure I was seeing things right.

As I walked over into the yard and peeked through the front window looking like a stalker the neighbor walked out saying. "Are you looking to buy this home? The owners just moved away last week."

I jumped and said, "No ma'am I was just checking the house out for a friend that's looking for a home." Knowing good and well I was lying.

"Oh well if your friend has a small family that will be a nice house for them. I am sorry my name is Marsha I live next door. I am really going to miss this family." Marsha said to me.

"I am sure you will. Did they say where they were moving to? I mean maybe they aren't too far you can still visit with them." I asked hoping for answers.

"No, Glinda didn't tell me. That was the wife's name. They just said they were moving away for a new start for the both of them."

"Sorry to hear that. You look like you really miss them." I said trying to sound concerned.

"Yes, I do. You know you look really familiar do I know you from somewhere?" She asked with a look as if she was trying to figure out where she had seen me before.

After looking into her face, I remembered her too. Glinda brought her to church with her last Christmas for her son Benny's

Christmas program. I had to hurry up and leave before she starts to remember. I didn't know how close she and Glinda were so I didn't know how much she knew about Bentley and me.

"No, I don't think I know you but hey it's been good talking to you. I better be going, I was in the neighborhood and saw this house and thought I would stop by to check it out." I reached out shook her hand and hurried away.

On my way home I swear I went through a half of pack of my Newport's. I pulled into my driveway and ran into the house and straight to my room. I felt like I was going to die. I guess this was how things were going to be from now on. I would just be one lonely missionary.

Months went by I started to feel like myself again. I had been letting these men get to me and I forgot all about God. I began to pray and ask God to order my steps because it was me that started this mess, once I started seeking God I got back in the church. I went before the church confessed my sins and ask for forgiveness.

Pastor Edwards counseled me for a while and gave me another chance to step up to be the woman of God had called me to be. Once William saw the woman I had become he slowly started coming back around to work on our marriage. I tell you I have put in overtime to prove to this man that I will be the woman he needs this time and he promised to be there for me as well. As for Bentley he never reached out to me and I never reached out to him anymore. That is a fling that is dead and buried forever.

Glinda

It has been a few months since Bentley and I moved to College Station, Texas and we couldn't be happier. Benny even noticed the change in our relationship. We started doing more thing as a family. Like one day when we took Benny to the Addison Lagoon Waterpark. This is something Bentley swore he never had time for.

We all went down to Wal-Mart to buy us some swimwear. Benny thought he was a little man so he got a pair of swim trunks to match his dad's. I, on the other hand, had to feel like such a lady. I got a black and pink one piece with a wraparound skirt to match it. I couldn't be showing all my Godly goods.

Bentley and Benny tried to get on everything they could. I sat back and watched with my feet in the water. I didn't want my hair to get wet. When we left the water park we were all starving we drove over to Golden Coral and tried to eat everything we could. We were so stuffed we had to sit back for a while and let our food digest.

Once we made it home Benny was so tired he was ready to shower and call it a day. Bentley and I decided that after our showers were done we would curl up on the couch and watch the movie "War Room." I had seen it before but Bentley hadn't so it was shocking to see how he cried from watching the things that happened in this movie.

"Bentley, I had to forgive you for two reasons and that's God and Benny. I couldn't go back on my vows I made before God and it would have torn Benny's world apart if I would have left you." I told him wiping the single tear away from my cheek that escaped my eye.

"Glinda, I never want to hurt you two again. If I never told you before you mean the world to me."

The Deacon and His First Lady   Tammy T. Cross

    I leaned over and gave him a kiss and said, "You better mean that because next time you may not be so lucky to be sitting here having a conversation with me." I told him letting out a jokingly laugh but deep inside really meaning it.

    The next morning, I got up and went to work while Bentley hung out at home with Benny. While I was at work my friend Lakita invited me to family and friends' day at her church. Lord knows I needed to get back to somebody's church with my family before the devil tries one of his tactics again.

    "Sure, I would love to go. I can't wait to share the news with my husband I am sure he will be just as excited as I am. Back where we come from he used to be the Deacon at the church." I informed Lakita.

    "Really well that's great he should fit right in then," Lakita said to me.

    "Well I better get going I got a patient down in room 1104 I think they say she was shot by her husband," I whispered to Lakita.

    "Oh, no well I better get going myself I am on the floor with the babies today so I should have it easy today and besides I love spoiling those folk's babies before I send them home with their mother's," Lakita said as she walked away laughing.

    I shook my head and walked to my room. "Hello Mrs. Warren, my name is Glinda I will be your nurse today. I am here to check your vitals. Can you sit up for me please?" I asked her while helping her to sit up a little in her bed.

    "Yes, ma'am and can you give me something for pain? I am hurting so bad. I don't know when the last time they gave me something," said Mrs. Warren.

    I looked at the charts and it was time for her to have her next dose of medication. "Yes ma'am, I will go get your medication right now," I told her as I took the blood pressure cup off her arm and made my way down to the nurse's station to order her next dose of medication.

    Ten minutes later I went back in with her medication and helped her to lie back down. "Mrs. Warren here is your buzzer; if you need anything else please don't hesitate to push the button," I told her as she laid back down with pain written all over her face.

    I walked out her room feeling so bad for her. I wanted to ask her so badly what had caused her injury but I didn't want to come off to nosey. I went around to each of my other patient's room one by one until my shift was over. Before I left I stopped back by Mrs. Warren's room and told her I was leaving for the day and if she was still there tomorrow I would see her when I came back in the morning.

    She thanked me for being so nice to her. I was about to walk out when God instructed me to pray for her. "Mrs., do you mind if I pray for you before I leave," I asked her.

    "Sure, go ahead," she said as she closed her eyes as if she was preparing for me to pray.

    "Father God I come today to ask for healing for Mrs. Warren. Lord, you know all about her and the things that she is going through. Lord, I ask that you take care of the person that has caused pain to her body. Lord give her a speedy recovery and make her whole once again. Lord, you spared her life and kept her here a little while longer and I thank you for letting this sweet lady live. Now from this day forward, I ask that you put your shield and protection around her and keep her safe from all hurt, harm, and danger in Jesus name Amen.

    "Mrs. Warren, you have a wonderful night and I will see you tomorrow," I told her before I walked out and headed home.

    When I made it home Bentley had grilled some ribs and prepared some baked beans and potato salad. I was starving so I washed up and headed right to the kitchen where Bentley had our plates all fixed up and a nice ice-cold glass of fruit punch juice. "So how was your day Babe?" Bentley asked as I join him and Bentley at the table.

    "It was great, my friend Lakita invited us to come to visit her church Sunday for family and friend's day and I told her we would come," I told him hoping I didn't overstep my boundaries by agreeing to go before speaking with my husband.

"That would be great. You never know we just may have found a new church home. I have been praying that we would find a church to attend soon because I miss being in the house of the Lord." He told me as a huge smile spread across my face.

When I saw the huge smile on his face it made me feel so good inside. I have been missing church but I also had a hard time thinking about going back to church. The reason for that is I didn't think that I could trust the women in the church after the last situation I was in with Bentley. Then I had to sit back and think to myself, really Glinda you need to check your man boo cause the women can't do any more than your man let them.

I thought about how things were going with us now that we moved away and thought I would give it another try. Besides this time if Ben even thought about looking at another woman he just may wake up with no man parts any longer. Oh, and the women of the church will know that Bentley belongs to me. I know that he's not all that but he belongs to me and only me. My friends are always telling me to leave his no good behind evidently, they knew he was cheating and didn't want to hurt my feeling but I love that man. I felt they didn't like him because of the way he looked but the real reason was the skeletons he had hiding way in the back of his closet.

Then next day it was my time to cook. I went and cleaned up and went to start dinner. I wanted a good old fashion home cooked meal. I prepared meatloaf, mash potatoes, green beans and we had some leftover cream cheese pound cake for dessert. I also took a few cokes out of the pantry and placed them in the freezer to get cool while I cooked.

When I was all done, we sat down to eat. Benny must have been really starved because we couldn't finish blessing the food good and he was shoving a fork full of meatloaf down his throat and washing it down with some of his coke. "Slow down Benny no one is going to take your food and if you want more there's plenty more where that came from. You are going to mess around and choke on that food, little boy." I fussed.

"Yes ma'am, I was just hungry I haven't eaten all day." He told me and I looked at Bentley with the meanest look on my face.

"You been here all day and you didn't feed my child Ben?" I asked him and he knew I was upset.

"Now Benny you make sure you tell your mom why you are hungry. Don't you just sit you're little behind there and make it seem like I didn't try to get you to eat." Bentley told Benny and waited for him to come clean with me.

"Benny is this true?" I asked him and he sat there looking at me like I never said a word. When he did that it made me feel so angry.

"Little boy if you don't answer me I will send you to bed without eating the rest of your dinner "I yelled out to him.

"Mom he asked me and I was playing my game and wasn't ready to eat yet." He finally admitted to me.

"I see that game has been taking up too much of your time. From now on you only get an hour and a half on that game a day. I need you to do better things with your time. So tomorrow I want you to find something else to do besides playing the game. I also want you to read the Bible at least an hour a day. Make use of that Bible I bought you a couple of years ago." I told him and I could see he didn't like it one bit but I didn't care.

He finished his food and asked to be excused from the table. When he got to the kitchen he rinsed out his plate and threw it in the dishwasher. Before I knew it, I jumped up and ran in that kitchen so fast you would have thought I was a strike of lighting.

"Little boy you must have lost your mind throwing my plate in the dishwasher like that. You keep up that attitude you going to be picking your teeth up off the floor. I am not what you want right now you understand me." I snapped at him, letting him know that I seriously meant what I said.

"Yes, ma'am." He replied and stormed off to his room looking like his dad and a mixture of me all in one.

"The nerve of that boy, Ben you better get your son before I have to put something on his backside. He is acting like that because he has a time limit on his game and gonna throw my plate you better let him know I am the mama and I mean just what I say." I rambled on while Ben looked at me like he was scared I was about to go in on him.

"Calm down Glinda what is going on with you. Seem like you got something else on your mind other than Benny throwing a plate in the dishwasher," Bentley said to me.

I must admit he was right. Lately, I have been having flashbacks of him and Gracie and it was bothering me tremendously. I didn't know how to tell him but I thought it was the time that he and I talk about it now.

"Bentley, I know we moved to start over but I can't get over how you cheated with Gracie. I sit back and wonder if you touched her like you touched me or did you give her your all and just played your part here with me just to get it over with." I manage to mumble out without breaking down. I then started to think I owed Benny an apology for yelling at him like I did.

Ben slid in close wrapped his arms around me and held me as he looked into my eyes a good minute before he spoke. It was as if he wanted to make sure he said the right thing before he opened his mouth to speak. "Glinda, I have told you a thousand times how sorry I am. I know the pain won't go away just like that but we promised each other that we would put what happened with Gracie and me in the past and moved forward."

"Yeah, Ben you are right but it is natural for a woman that has given you her all and still not do enough for her husband, so he goes and finds comfort in another woman." I pulled away from him now starting not to even wanting him touching me.

"Glinda, I didn't find comfort in another woman. There was nothing wrong with you. I just let the flesh take over me. You see the devil know how to send people your way and it causes you to do wrong. The devil is a flea baby and he must flee because I need our relationship to get back on track." Ben said to me causing me to laugh at his lil twisted joke when I didn't even want to laugh.

I got up from the table and went to apologize to my son for being so hard on him. "Benny, mama need to talk to you for a moment?"

"Yes, Ma'am," he responded as he wiped the tears from his eyes. I guess I really hurt his feelings for him to be still crying.

"I came to say sorry for yelling at you the way I did. Mama has been going through some things lately and I guess I kind of took it out on you." I pulled him close to me as we sat at the foot of his little bunk bed.

"I know mama I hear you and daddy arguing from time to time." I stopped and looked at him hurt at what he had just told me.

"Oh, Benny I never meant for you to hear that. You know sometimes parents go through things and it causes them to fuss but we still love each other. It was just a little disagreement baby." I rubbed his head and said.

"Mama, can I ask you a question and do you promise to be honest with me? I am eleven years old now and I am old enough to know what's going on." I shook my head yes, all at the same time scared of the question he was going to ask.

"Did daddy really have an affair with the lady down at the church?" He asked and I felt like I was going to pass out before I could even answer him.

"Baby, now that is something that you don't need to worry about." I tried to tell him hoping he would let it go.

"Mama you promised you would answer. So, did he do it or not?" He asked me now looking upset.

I looked up and silently asked God for help. I looked at the door to see if Ben was standing there listening but he wasn't. "Yes, Benny he did," I started saying before he jumped up off the bed and started toward the room where his daddy was yelling "I am going to kill him."

I jumped up and scooped his little boney behind up and sat him right back on the bed. "Benny that is your father and you will not disrespect him or I. Do you understand me, lil boy?"

"Yes ma'am" he responded.

"Now you leave grown folk's business to me and go take a shower and get your behind in the bed." I grabbed him and hugged him before he ran over to the drawer and pulled out his favorite pair of PJ's and a pair of boxers before heading to the bathroom."

When he left out of the room I sit there a little while longer and shed a few tears before I pulled myself together and headed back to the living room where Benny was watching TV.

Bentley

Standing at the door listening to my wife talk to my son really hurt me to my soul. Hearing my wife telling my son I had an affair and him expressing his hate for me had me feeling sick in the stomach. The hard part was him trying to come for me. I did it to myself and I can't blame anyone but myself for how he feels toward me. He defended me at school and to find it was true had to cut to the core.

Benny walked through the living going to the bathroom and instead of stopping to talk to me like all the time before, he just gave me an evil looked and kept walking. I wanted to snatch his little behind up and let him know that I am still his daddy and he will show me some respect but I let him make it this time since he was hurting. Later, we will have a father-son talk.

Glinda came back in the room trying to wipe her face clean and pretending things were alright but I knew better. "Glinda, come sit right here for a minute," I said as I patted the spot next to me on the couch.

"Benny knows the truth, Bentley." She said breaking down as she sat down next to me.

"I know I was standing at the door and heard everything." Letting her know I heard the whole conversation.

"The child is hurting and I think that is why he has started to act out. Benny has never acted in such a way or smarted off like that. He knows I don't play and I will plant my foot so far up his behind he would be able to smell it," she ranted on.

"I will handle it like I said before I am going to talk with Benny soon," I told her.

"He does not want to talk to you right now. With him being so upset with you he will only try to attack you to make you feel the pain he is feeling," she replied.

"He will listen to me," I shouted out in anger.

"So, you try to tell me to calm down and you the one getting angry now. If you would have just kept that gummy worm in your pants my family wouldn't be suffering now." Glinda shouted as she jumped up walking to her room slamming the door behind her.

I knew that if she walked off slamming the door behind her this meant that I would have to resort to my second bed tonight. I walked over to the hall closet grabbed the spare pillow and blanket out and made myself comfortable on the couch.

Sunday was here before we knew it; after breakfast was over we headed over to the church to hear the word of God. It felt so good to be sitting back in the house of the Lord. My family even seemed a little happier. The pastor preached so hard his whole face was covered in sweat. His sermon was about adultery out of all topics. I guess it was meant for me to be at today's service.

When service was over Lakita took us, and introduced us to her Pastor. He then invited us to come back and visit again. Before he could finish I shouted, "We would love to," speaking for me and my family before I knew it.

"Pastor Elton chuckled and said, "Well I will see you guys next Sunday, shook each of our hands and went on to conversate with the rest of the members.

Glinda and I let Kita know just how much we enjoyed the service. While Benny chopped it up with her son Trey. I didn't want to stare at her much because I didn't want Glinda to think I was checking for her friend. I had to admit that she was a nice-looking woman she was a beautiful milk chocolate big bone woman with light brown eyes. she stood about five-foot-six weighing 175 pounds. Her hips were so perfect and round the next female would say she had butt injections. Her breast was sitting so high that when she laughed they jiggled so hard I thought they were going to pop out of her low-cut dress.

I walked off so that the women could talk. I passed by a few people and introduced myself. I started a conversation about today's sermon with a couple of guys that were standing in the corner chatting while their wives were engaged in a conversation of their own with other women in the church.

Glinda was ready to go, we thanked Kita for the invite and said our goodbyes and drove home. My son looked happier than he did in weeks. I think he enjoyed chopping it up with Trey as much as Glinda did with her girl Kita. I decided that since the day was going so well we would end it by going to Sodolaks Steak House in Bryan for a nice dinner.

Benny was doing so well coping with playing his game an hour a day that Glinda agreed while we went on outings or road trips he could bring along his hand-held game. When we sat down and ordered our food he played while Glinda and I discussed today's sermon. "The pastor really did preach a good sermon today didn't he babe." I picked up my glass of water the waiter brought to the table for us and listened to her express how much she needed to hear the message that Pastor Elton gave today.

"Oh, my what a word, what a word. It feels like he was sending a message straight to my heart. He said things that helped me in so many ways. When he started talking about the way God wants us to forgive others. I silently said, *Lord you got to be talking to me.*"

The waitress came and brought our food and I instructed Benny to put away his game so that I could bless the food and we could eat. "Heavenly Father I want to thank you for all that you have done for us today. I thank you for leading us to a wonderful church service and meeting new people that love the lord as much as we do. Lord I also want you to bless this food that we are about to receive. I pray that it is nourishing to our bodies. In Jesus name, Amen."

All I could hear was, "Amen" coming from my wife and Benny following forks clicking on plates. I looked around the table and thought about how lucky I was to have a family like I have.

The Deacon and His First Lady   Tammy T. Cross

Things may not be back like it used to be but thank God it is not torn up like it was in the past.

    When dinner was over the family and I drove home. We were all stuffed from dinner so we didn't have much to say on the ride home. We let the windows down and let some fresh cool air in as we listen to the late Timothy Wright sing his heart out. Glinda had to be feeling every hymn he sang because all I could see was her hand in the air and her bobbing her head from side to side.

    When we arrived back at the house we all went in changed into something comfortable. Glinda went in and finished the laundry that she started the day before. She then told Benny to get his room cleaned and I decided to go to the study and read my bible for a little while. I felt like I had gotten off track and now is the time I get my life back together.

    After reading my word I thought I needed to go have a conversation with my son after I overheard the conversation he had with my wife, it had me in my feelings. I knew by the way he was talking he was hurt because I cheated on him as well as my wife. I owe this talk to him and now is the best time to do it.

    I walked up to his room door and peeked in before I knocked. He was busy cleaning his room. When I saw, he put away the last shirt his mom had just given him from the laundry I knocked. "Come in," he yelled without turning around to see who it was.

    "Hey son, can you sit down for a minute so we can talk?" I asked while patting the spot on the bed next to me.

    "Sure dad, what's going on," he said as he sat down next to me on the bed.

    "I know you have heard bad things that I have done to your mom and you. I don't have an excuse for what I did but I can't change that either. All I can do is say that I am sorry for hurting you two. I also hope that you can find it in your heart to forgive me." I said as I tried to read the blank expression that was written on his chocolate face.

    "Dad I can't believe you did that with Mrs. Gracie. Kids teased me every day at school. I feel like a complete fool because I defended you for the rumors to turn out to be true. Dad, you hurt me," he said as tears began to stream down his little cheeks.

I lean in to give my son a hug and let him know I have changed but he didn't give the reaction I expected. He jumped up and yelled, "I hate you, get away from me and don't touch me you are a cheating dog."

Glinda came running into the room to see what all the commotion was about. I don't know why but him talking to me in such a way really upset me. I just wanted to snatch him up and give him a good butt whooping. I know I had it coming but I am his daddy and he will not disrespect me like that.

"What in the world is going on in here? Ben let Benny go you are hurting him. Now I don't know what y'all got going on but this has got to stop and stop right now. Glinda said as she stepped in and grabbed Benny out of my hands.

"I am sorry you guys I lost it. I only wanted to apologize for hurting you guys but when he went off on me like he did I couldn't take it." I said as I lowered my head in shame.

I understand Ben but grabbing him like that is not a way to react. You were wrong just as much as Benny was. Let's just go into the den and all three of us have a talk." Glinda suggested.

Benny still huffing and puffing led the way to the den. Glinda started the conversation off by talking to Benny. "Look, baby, your daddy was wrong for stepping out on us like he did but that is still your daddy. Now as long as you live you don't ever disrespect him like you did tonight do you understand Benny?" Glinda told him in a demanding voice.

"Yes Ma'am," he said in a low voice.

"You Bentley should know better. I know you upset and all but trying to discipline him for his reaction to you telling him you cheated, man what did you expect him to do. He almost had fights daily defending you and now to find out you really did do what those kids said you did. How do you think he feels? Really, Ben, you should know better," fussed Glinda.

"Look I am sorry to the both of you. Every time I try to do better it seems as if I just keep failing you two. I don't know what to say but I am trying my best to make it up to you two. I know I can't take back what I did but I can just do better than what I did and hope for forgiveness." I looked at my wife and son's eyes showing all the pain that I was holding inside of me.

Glinda reached in and gave me a hug and Benny came in behind her and hugged me as well. It made me feel good inside because we started out having a wonderful day and I didn't want the devil to ruin it. We sat and talked it over a little while longer before we turned in for the night.

After everyone was fast asleep I couldn't rest well so I eased out of bed and slid on my house shoes and sat at the kitchen table and had a little one on one with God. I opened up to him about everything I was going through and at that moment I could feel relief covering my entire body. I felt as if God was right there with me and was helping me overcome the pain that I was feeling for hurting my family. After talking to God for several hours I thought it was time I crawl back into bed before my wife notice that I was gone.

Glinda

It has been months since our little family altercation. We've been going to church with Kita every Sunday since then. Benny's attitude has changed so much for the better. He and Trey have become so close that every chance they get they would link up and hang out for hours at a time. I think it's a good thing because now he doesn't spend as much time on that dang PlayStation 4. The exciting part about the whole thing is that the pastor asked Bentley to be the deacon at House of Repentance C.O.G.I. C. and he accepted the position.

That Sunday the pastor announced Bentley as a deacon and let him get up before the congregation and say a few words. I could tell he was a little nervous but he did great. He sounds like he did when he uses to bring the message back in the days when we were at the church in Somerville. Thanks to my friend Kita inviting us to her church I can now say I feel comfortable sitting in the house of the Lord one more time as the ole saints would say in their testimony.

Bentley started working with Sharon Stone putting programs together and trying to start a business helping people in need about six months of us joining the church. It was hard for me to deal with in the beginning but after months of them working together, I finally became comfortable with it. I knew how sorry he was for cheating on me the last time and trusted that he would never hurt me nor Benny ever again.

I worked my four days on for the week and was now on my two days off. Boy, it sure felt good to get Benny off to school and kick back and prop my feet up on the couch. I planned on spending my whole day catching up on the latest new book releases. There was one I had been waiting on for a month called When Daddy's Gone by a young lady name Mekiyah N. Boone. When I tell you that book was so good I couldn't put it down. An hour later I had read that entire book. I must say to be so young she is one talented little girl. I hear her mother is also an author with wonderful books. That goes to show kids learn from some of the things they learn from their parents. That is why I try to tell my husband we must live right before our child if we want him to live a good lifestyle.

After reading her book I read another book by an author that was based on her life. I got so caught up in that book I had let time get away from me and almost forgot about getting up to prepare dinner for my son and husband. I closed it up until later because that book was so deep nothing was going to stop me from going back to finish reading it.

I walked into the kitchen and took the steaks out of the sink that was thawing out and washed them off before I seasoned them. I then set them to the side while I washed three big potatoes off, poked a hole in them on both sides and wrapped them in foil. I grabbed a cookie sheet out of the cabinet and placed them in the oven on 350 degrees. Picking up the charcoal, lighter fluid and matches up out of the bottom of the pantry I headed out my kitchen door that led to my backyard.

When I reached the end of my patio I reached up and opened my grill top to make sure Bentley had cleaned it off the last time we grilled on it and I shouldn't have been surprised because he always has a habit of cleaning it off the moment we are done with it. "Yes, Lord I don't have to clean it," I said to myself smiling as I loaded the pit with the charcoal. I then pour some lighter fluid on the coal, lit it and watched it burn until it was just like I wanted it.

Once I got my steaks and put them in the pit. I thought since today was such a pretty cool and windy day I would sit out on the back patio and finish reading the book I started. As soon as I got into it good I could have sworn I heard my name being called. I laid my book down and looked around and said, "Lord I know I ain't going crazy."

A few moments later I heard it again and it was even closer so I stood up and walked in the house and it was Bentley he had come home early since I was off to spend a little time with me on my off day. "Oh, my Bentley you scared the life out of me. For a minute, there I thought I was going crazy." I told him standing there with my hand across my chest, while my heart was pounding so fast.

"Girl you are standing there holding your heart like you thought it was judgement day and Jesus was calling your name to step up next." Bentley chuckled and jokily said.

"Bentley stop it you just kill me with the stuff that comes out your mouth," I said as I walked up to him and hug him while kissing him on the cheek at the same time.

Holding me in his bony arms he asked me, "What have you been doing all day sweetheart?"

"Just doing a little reading on some of the books that I have missed out on. You know me I love to read and every chance I can break away you will find me with a book in my hands."

"Yes, that is true I don't know why I asked that question," Bentley replied as he looked in the direction of the grill.

A few minutes later he pulled away and walked over to the grill and lift the top to see what I had cooking. "Steaks, good lord I must be in heaven because you only cook these on special occasions." He said as he rubbed his hands across his stomach.

I looked at him and my insides felt a hurt that I haven't felt in a long time. He looked away as if he didn't notice the look on my face. I grabbed my book off the table and my glass of lemonade and walked into the house to check on my bake potatoes in the oven. I tell you when I walked into the house and made it to the kitchen I had already let a few tears escape my eyes. I couldn't control them from flowing.

A few minutes later I heard Bentley enter the house behind me. I tried to clear the water from my eyes before he made it over to the oven where I was bent over pushing the potatoes back inside the oven. "What is wrong sweetheart looks like you are upset about something? Come on let's go sit in the living room and talk about it." Bentley then grabbed my hand and led me to the living room area.

The moment I walked into the room my eyes lit up like I was in Vegas. Bentley has done it once again. He has flowers, a huge teddy bear, and a big balloon that read Happy Anniversary. The biggest smile rolled across my face and the waterworks began to flow. "Bentley, I thought you had forgotten our Anniversary. When you rolled out of bed, cleaned up and kiss me and left this morning I just knew you didn't remember." I told him as I grabbed him and hugged him so tight.

"Wait a minute now mama bear you know I am a fragile thing and easy to break in half you can't be holding me like that." He said as he wiggled his way out of the death grip I had on him.

"Boy, you just comical today but I should have known you hadn't forgotten. Out of all the years we have been together I can't think of a year you ever did. This year I think it was different because of how you just left this morning without saying much of nothing to me." I told him

"Well before you start talking my ear off sit down I got one more gift for you," Bentley told me

He reached into his right jacket pocket and pulled out a bright gold box. As I opened it I kept my eyes on the big smile on his face. When I pulled the top off there was a big beautiful diamond ring down in the box. Bentley reached and pulled my old wedding ring off and replaced it with the new ring in the box. He then leaned in and kissed my lip and I felt just like a young girl all over again.

We sit and chatted for a moment until I remembered I had some steaks on the grill. Bentley looked at me crazy when I jumped up and ran out the back door like a strike of lighting. I yanked open the grill and took a deep breath when I saw they were just fine, I picked up my tongs and flipped them over. Bentley then joins me outside with two glasses of lemonade. We sit and enjoyed the day laughing and talking on the patio until our steaks were done.

As I took the steaks off the grill and the potatoes out of the oven Bentley drove over to the school to pick up Benny while I made a salad and a fresh pitcher of homemade lemonade. When Benny made it home Bentley helped him with his homework. Once he was done he was starving. "Go wash up guys and when you return I will have your plates fixed and on the table," I yelled out to them.

Since Benny been in this world we have never celebrated our anniversary without him. Not only is this a special day for us it is also one for him. A couple of years after we were married Benny was born on the day we got married so we all celebrate together every year. When we finished eating dinner Bentley and I gave Benny his birthday gift. The first gift was a box with three games for his PlayStation and the next one we didn't know how he will react when he opens it.

"A children's bible mom you and dad just don't know how bad I wanted one of these. I tried to read the one you guys got me like yours but I didn't understand what some of the stuff meant," shouted Benny

"Well, son that one you shouldn't have a problem reading because it is a bible that is designed for kids like you to read," Bentley told Benny as he stood up and helped him carry his gifts to his room.

When Ben returned I had just finished clearing the kitchen and starting up the dishwasher. I walked over to the couch and sit down beside him. "Honey before this night ends I got a gift for you," I said as I pulled the box from behind my back.

Ben took the gift from my hand and said, "Glinda you shouldn't have." All while tearing into the wrapper that I had on the small box.

When he pulled the Apple watch out of the box I could have sworn I see a tear forming up in his eye. When he grabbed me and landed a long kiss on my lips I knew I did well picking out this gift."

When he kissed me like that he made my knees weak. Bentley hadn't kissed me like that in a very long time. I knew that was a kiss that was filled with love. "Boy, now that's how Benny got here you better watch it." I laughed and said to him.

"You keep on giving me gifts like this we are going to have another Benny girl," he said as he smacked me on my behind.

"Stop it now Ben you got some strength behind that hit that kind of hurt boy," I told him as I rubbed my backside.

Ben and I lay around on the couch and enjoyed each other's company for a few hours before I got up and made sure Benny had taken his bath and was in bed for the night. I walked back out and Ben and I decided that we would grab another glass of lemonade and enjoy the rest of the beautiful night curled up in the back-yard rocking on the hammock that was connected to two big trees in the backyard, while reminiscing on old times and gazing at the stars in the big star-filled sky.

Sharon

Working down at the church brings so much joy to my life. Whenever I am in the house of the lord I feel so much closer to God. I stay at the church working on projects so much; the pastor has to make me go home to my family. I told him," Pastor, working keeps me stress-free."

"He then told me, "child keep living you ain't seen stress yet." I let out a laugh and grabbed my bags and headed home to my family.

My husband Nova is a wonderful hard-working man. He does everything in his power to make sure our two children don't want for anything. That brown-skinned, six-foot-seven, hazel-eyed man, has been had my heart for twelve long years. From the way, he wears his hair cut close in a bald fade, to his medium size frame body. Oh, and his beautiful perfect white teeth makes this five foot four, 146-pound slim thick woman, falls head over heels in love with him every time he smiles. His friends gave him the nickname Will Smith because they say he acts so much like him but he looked a spitting image of R. Kelly. They call me Kandi Burrus because my friends say I look and sound like her so much it is kind of scary.

I have two beautiful children Caleb and Kara. Caleb is the baby of the family he is six and looks so much like me. Kara is ten years old and looks so much like her daddy; one would think he spit her out himself instead of me. The only thing Kara took from me is my spunky personality. Caleb, on the other hand, is chill and laid back like Nova. One thing about Nova and me we always vowed to keep our children in church and teach them all about the goodness of the lord. So far, I must say we have done a great job.

While working down at the church, I have met some great people. A matter of fact we have a new wonderful deacon name

The Deacon and His First Lady — Tammy T. Cross

Bentley that I have had the pleasure of working closely with lately. I haven't had the pleasure of talking with his wife much but my son is crazy about their son Benny. Benny is older than my son but Caleb feels like a big boy when he gets to hang out with him. That part I enjoy because for a long time Caleb was always acting like a baby. Nova told me a long time ago that all he needed was another male close to his age, to hang out with, and he would grow out of it. Now I see that he was right about that. I guess you can say it was my fault a little bit, because I knew I wasn't going to have any more kid's, due to the fact I had gotten my tubes tied, clipped and burnt, so I wanted to enjoy my baby as long as possible.

    Bentley and I had started spending so much time at the church together, that we became very close to one other. I could talk to him about anything, and he felt the same about me. When we were not at the church and Glinda wasn't working we started having dinner at each other's house from time to time like one big family.

    Kara felt a little out of place because she didn't have any girls her age to play with. We often brought along her friend Symone, she also was a member of our church. That made Kara happy because she had someone she could talk with.

    I was sitting on the couch thinking about new ideas to make our business for the church a success. I couldn't think of any new ideas right now, so I just got up and threw on a nice pink and white sundress, and some white sandals that had a beautiful little pink flower on the top of them. I always did like pretty girly things. Dressing like this made me feel like a princess. I even dress Kara like me sometimes. We would have matching dresses and shoes. I think Kara like the idea of dressing alike more than I did.

    "Hey princess, you are looking beautiful today," Nova said as he scooped me up into his arms for a nice morning kiss.

    "Thank you, babe," I replied and twirled around like I know I was killing it in my sundress.

    Nova doesn't comment me much so when he did I know I had to be looking extra cute. I grabbed my purse and keys and headed out the door and over to the church. I wanted to go see if

Bentley has come up with any new ideas for the business. I made it to the church and pulled down the sun visor to see if I had any lip gloss left on my lips from the kiss Nova planted on me earlier. I reached into my purse and pulled the tube of gloss out, and applied a little more before I got out and made my way inside the church.

I walked to the pastor's office he was nowhere to be found so I went over the deacon's office and found Bentley looking over some paper he had on his desk. "Hey Ben," I blurted out scaring him so badly that the paper he was reading fell out of his hand.

"Sharon, you startled me, and you are looking really nice today. What's the occasion?" He asked looking at me like I was a juicy steak. I didn't know if I was enjoying the stare more than being surprised at him.

"Uhmm, there is no occasion" I stuttered hoping my words would come out right. I just woke up in a good mood today and thought I would throw on a nice comfortable dress I had hanging in the back of my closet." I strolled over to sit in the chair that was across from him at his desk.

The whole time I was making my way to the chair Bentley never took his eyes off me and it was as though I could read every thought he had in his head. I tried to change the mood in the room by asking him a question because I knew his thoughts of me were wrong and feeling I was having at this moment was wrong as well.

"How has Glinda and Benny been?" I asked as he gathered the papers in a neat pile. That was a mess because of me walking in starling him.

"Oh uhmm, Glinda and Benny are great," he mumbled out as if his nerves were getting the best of him.

"Bentley are you ok? You seem to be sweating hard, are you not feeling well today. I asked as I grabbed a napkin from the windowsill passing it over to Ben.

"No, I am feeling well," he told me as he grabbed the napkin dabbing the sweat from his face. "I think it's just a little warm in this church. The maintenance man hasn't arrived yet to service the AC unit."

"Well now that you mentioned it, it is a little warm in here," I said as I removed the vest I had on to cover my shoulders that kept my arms from being too exposed.

"I-I will be right back. Would you like a bottle of water from the cafeteria?" Bentley asked me as he hurried out of the office not waiting for an answer.

I wasn't sure if I was the cause of him to be acting so strange but if we are going to get any work done he is going to have to loosen up a bit. While he was gone I walked over to the window and raised it up enough for me to fit the fan he had sitting in the corner in it. After a few minutes, I could feel a difference in the room. The air that was circulating the room felt so good and smelled so fresh.

"Wow! I never thought about putting that old fan in the window like that. It feels a hundred percent better than before. I remember as a child when my mom uses to place our fans in the window to cool the house down. You know how we use to do it back in the days without central air and heat right Sharon," he joked.

"Hey old man I don't know what you are talking about I am not as old as you," I giggled and snapped back.

He chuckled back saying, "now you know you are in the house of the lord let me sit back before lighting comes flashing down on you."

"Boy, have a seat over there and let's get started on this project or we will never accomplish anything today," I pointed at his chair across the desk from him and said.

An hour later Pastor Elton came in to see what we were working on. The ideas that Ben had about helping the needy, really impressed him. "Bentley, man you are a genius. If we could have come up with these ideas years ago we could have helped the needed and made extra cash for the church." Pastor shouted as he patted Bentley on his back.

"I can't take all of the credit for this Pastor Elton; Sharon had a part in this too," replied Ben as he stood up to shake the pastor's hand.

Sharon knows I appreciate her. If I didn't she would have been gone years ago. She has been one of the best things that happened to The House of Repentance. When you came I pair you two together because I felt like both of you guys working together would bring nothing but greatness to our church and thanks to God, you two proved just that." He said as he walked around and hugged me before he exited the room.

    Bentley and I worked about thirty minutes longer before we decided to call it quits for the day. We walked out to the church parking lot and said our goodbyes before we both headed in our own directions. I drove down highway 6 listening to the radio chattering away about different celebrities and things they are going through. I didn't care to hear anything about Jay Z and Queen B so I turn it down to ride silently. After a ten-minute ride, I finally made it home. Nova was at work and the kids were still at school. So, I went in plopped down on the couch and kicked my feet up to relax for a while before starting dinner.

Bentley

Leaving the church, I had a lot on my brain. I knew that if I wanted Glinda to trust me again I had to keep thing under control. Being around Sharon I was like Adam was when it came to Eve and I know that couldn't happen with us. I sent up a quick prayer and ask the Lord to control us when we are each other's presences. I can tell by the look in her eyes that she saw the look I gave her when I saw her in that dress.

Before I knew it, I was pulling up in my driveway. I got out of my car and walked in the house where Glinda was preparing dinner and jamming "God Is Good" by Deitrick Haddon. She was swaying from side to side so hard she didn't even hear me walk up behind her. Before she knew it, I was standing behind her holding up her waist and swaying with her.

"Oh, Ben you scared the devil out of me. I didn't even hear you come in." She told me turning around giving me a kiss on my cheek.

"If Detrick wouldn't have all your attention, you would have heard me. He gets more attention than me. Every time I get in your car that is all I hear." I said trying to sound as if I was jealous.

"You are silly Ben, but uh let's not get started on you and Yolanda Adams. Naw honey do not go tipping out of here now. You are all up in the car saying," "*I open up my heart to you.*" She mocked me to the T. I could just hear myself singing it.

"You know what you got me on that one I am just going to go have a seat in the living room until dinner is served," I told her in my Leroy Brown voice.

Glinda laughed as I walked out of the kitchen. I sat down on the sofa and turned the television on CNN. I heard about a terrorist attack that happened in New York and I begin to pray for the people that were involved in the attack. I must have fallen asleep because I was awakened by Benny coming through the door talking to his mother all about the things he did at school.

"He Benny you don't see nobody but your mother," I raised up off the couch saying as I threw a plush pillow at him to get his attention.

"Daddy! I didn't see you over there. How was your day today down at the church.?" He asked as he ran and jumped on the couch with me like he was excited to see me.

"Hold on now you ain't-a baby anymore you are too big to be jumping all on me like that," I said trying to change the subject about my day because it sent a flashback in my head of Sharon in that sundress.

"Sorry old man but you didn't tell me how your day went?" Benny brought the subject back up and I tried to get Sharon off my mind and give him a quick answer.

"Well it went pretty good, I came up with some great ideas to help the needy as well as the church. I must inform you that Pastor Elton was very pleased with it too. Now looks like mommy is done with dinner lets go wash our hands and go to the table, I am starving."

I went to the bathroom next to my room to wash my hands to get out of the room to clear my head. As I walked out I saw Glinda standing in the kitchen giving me a concerned stare. I tell you that woman could read a snake if she had to. I don't know what it is about her but I had to pull it together before I get back to the dinner table because we have come so far, I didn't want her to lose trust in me again.

I came back out to the table and Glinda and Benny were sitting down waiting for me to join them. "Sorry I took so long but I had to use the bathroom as well. Come on bow your heads and let's pray. *Father God, I ask that you bless this food so that it will be for the nourishing of our bodies. Bless the hands that prepared it and thank you Lord for allowing us to have food to eat. There are some that are less fortunate but we were blessed enough to have this meal. Lord, we can't thank you enough, in Jesus name Amen.*"

"Benny let's see if your mama still got it. We haven't had a nice home cooked meal from her in a while." I tried to get a reaction out of her by telling a joke.

"Hey now I have been working a lot of hours lately and you two should be happy to have gotten this meal. If I wouldn't have had a taste for these smothered oxtails, yams and broccoli and cheese casserole, we would have just been eating chili dogs and chips," Glinda laughed out and said.

"Well thank the Lord for your taste," shouted Benny causing all of us to burst into laughter.

Glinda thought that his comment was so funny she couldn't eat her food. I could tell she wasn't in her feelings about anything so I chimed in and joined the conversation and enjoy our nice family dinner. We laughed and joked a little longer and decided we'd better eat before our food was cold. When we were done Benny and I cleared the table and cleaned the kitchen so that Glinda could go kick back and relax.

After we were all done in the kitchen Benny went to his room to hang out likes he does all the time. I went to the living room to sit and spend some alone time with my wife. She was sitting back on the couch with her feet stretched out. I walked around and lifted her legs, slid her shoes off and started to massage her feet.

"So how was your day down at the hospital today honey?" I asked her as she tilted her head back like I had just hit the right spot on her foot.

"It was pretty slow today Ben and we were overstaffed for some reason today. Since I had been working so much over time I was able to leave early," she replied I grabbed her other foot and started massaging it.

"It worked out perfect, you and I get to spend some alone time together tonight and that's something we haven't got to do in a long time," I told her and she agreed.

We laid back on the couch and enjoyed each other like never before. I was enjoying my wife so much that I thought that we should move from the living room to the comfort of our bedroom in case one thing leads to another. I got up and grabbed her hand and led her to the bedroom where we laughed, talked and showed affection toward one another.

Glinda

I really enjoyed my husband's company so much last night that I didn't want to go to work but I knew there was money to be made. I woke up early this morning and took a nice shower leaving Ben asleep. The warm water rolling down the center of my back felt so good. I had been in the shower so long the water was starting to get cold. I stepped out of the shower grabbing my towel off the rack to dry off. When I peeked at the clock that was sinking by the sink, I knew that if I didn't hurry I would be late for work.

Once I got my Minnie Mouse scrubs on, I rushed into the kitchen to get me a cup of coffee. "Hey honey, I tried to slip out without waking you. I even ironed Benny's clothes for church and they are lying on the ironing board." I said as I grabbed the coffee he had made for me, along with a bacon and egg sandwich to eat on the run.

"I wanted to kiss my beautiful wife before you lift for work if that's fine with you," Ben said making his way to me.

"No baby it's perfectly fine it's just that you were resting so well I didn't want to wake you. Tell Pastor Elton sorry I couldn't make it to church today because I had to work." I kissed him and rushed out the door so I would make it to work on time.

I was driving down Hwy 6 trying to get to work I said a quick prayer for my family and for a good day. I then turned on the radio to listen to the Sunday morning gospels and Brian Courtney Wilson was on singing "All I Need." If I tell you that song got to me so bad, when I made it to work I couldn't get out of the car. I was in tears and praising God with everything in me. I finally pulled myself together cleaned my face, reapplied my makeup and walked in the job with a smile on my face.

My friend Kita wasn't at work today so I pulled my hair down over my ears and slid my earbuds in. I turn the music down low so that I could hear the things around me. I didn't get the

The Deacon and His First Lady Tammy T. Cross

pleasure of working with the babies today but I guess God had a better plan for my day. I went to my first patients' room and it was a 70-year-old lady name Mrs. Lula Mae Baker. Lula Mae was getting out of bed and became dizzy and took a nasty fall that left her with a broken hip.

"Good morning Mrs. Baker, I am Glinda your nurse for today. I am going to start out by checking your vitals." I informed her while placing her arm in the blood presser cup.

"Hey, baby how are you feeling today?" You are walking in here shinning like the star that was shining over baby Jesus," she said letting out a soft laugh.

I laughed and asked, "now why would you say that Mrs. Baker," As I documented her vitals on my clipboard, and unstrapped her blood pressure cup?

"I am an old saint and us older heads can tell a Christian by their walk and baby when you walk through that door I felt the spirit of the Lord walk in with you," she looked me dead in my eyes and said with a straight face.

I couldn't do anything but let out the tears that I had been fighting back so hard. "I am sorry Mrs. Lula but this is so unprofessional of me. I have to be honest with you before I came in I was listening to a song on the radio and I got so caught in the spirit I could hardly get out the car."

"Baby there is nothing unprofessional about letting the Lord have his way in your life. No matter where you are, you should always let your light shine. A lot of young folks think that there is a special place that you should serve the Lord. I serve him anywhere I feel his presences. Don't be a shame, the Lord said *but whosoever shall deny me before men, he will I also deny before my father who is in heaven.*"

I stood back and thought about what Mrs. Lula just said and I must admit she was right. One thing I couldn't understand is how this old lady knew I was a Christian just by looking at me. If I didn't believe you can tell a believer by their walk I was a believer now.

"I don't mean to change the subject but I have to go so that I can check out my next patient. I have one thing I need to know before I go how is your pain level on a scale of 1-10 with 10 being the worse?" I asked her while waiting for her to give me an answer.

"I will say it is about a six. I was hurting bad earlier and the other nurse came in about 10 minutes before you came and gave me some medication. I think it is kicking in because I feel the pain easing off and asleep coming over me." Lula told me talking and nodding off a little at the same time.

I let out a giggled and walked out trying to let her get some rest but I was amazed one minute she was talking to me about the lord and the next she was half asleep. She was such a sweet lady and I definitely had to go back to her room and chat with her before I left for the day.

I eased the door shut and walked out and pulled my next chart. I walked two doors down and knocked on the door of room 234." Come in" a deep voice hollered out.

"Hello Mr. Nathan Pillar, how are you feeling? I am Glinda your nurse for today; First off I would like to start by checking your vitals." I told him as I checked his armband to make sure it matched his paperwork.

"Hey yourself and don't be pulling on my arm so hard. What are you trying to do break it?" He yelled out pulling his arm from my hand.

"I am sorry Mr. Pillar I didn't mean to hurt your arm. I see you are in here because your blood pressure is extremely high. Do you take any medications for it?" I ask watching him roll his beady little eyes as if I was getting on his nerves.

"I am so tired of answering all of these questions. Everyone asking question after question, hell look at the charts and read what they wrote down." His little old Colt 45/Newport smelling behind shouted out at me.

"Mr. Pillar I am just doing my job I have to ask these questions and if you want us to help you, then you are going to have to cooperate with us," I informed him as I felt the old me surfacing. I had to tell the devil he was a lie, I took a deep breath and tried a different approach.

I looked at his charts and read everything I could possibly read to keep from asking him any more questions. Upon reading his charts I saw that the nurse before me had a hard time getting anything out of him so I sent up a silent prayer to the man up above and tried again. "I was just reading your charts and I see that you didn't give them any information on yourself. I will have to ask you again; do you take any medication for your blood pressure."

This time it was as if I was talking to a different person. "Yes, ma'am I do take medication. I take Lisinopril and I been on it for going on five years now and the doses are 5mg."

"Have you ever had a heart attack before?" I know that sometimes when its 5mg some people have had a heart attack." I ask not expecting his next answer.

"Has your mammy had a heart attack before? I am getting really sick of you people walking in hear asking me all my personal business. Go ask your mother if she had a heart attack and what medicine she on due to your daddy being a rolling stone and cheating on her trifling behind."

"Look, old man, my mother did happen to have a heart attack and it wasn't behind a no-good man like you. That mouth you got is the reason your mothball smelling, drunk behind in here now. Now if you don't start acting like you got some since I am going to…. "I had snapped and remembered I was at work and stop and apologize to the man.

"I am sorry I didn't mean to go off on you like that and I hope you forgive me for calling you out your name. I am going to go and get your medication because your blood pressure is elevated a bit." I turned to walk out to go get his medicine and this fool threw his breakfast cup and hit me with it. I turned around so fast and gave him a look scared the devil back to hell. If I tell you he was laughing so hard I had to turn and walk away before I broke him down to a fraction.

The Deacon and His First Lady   Tammy T. Cross

I walked out the door and realized that the devil was trying to steal my joy. I took a short break and went to the lady's room and prayed that God would send me peace of mind. Right now, this man got me thinking about putting something in his IV and sending him on to glory. The rage I was feeling for him was not of God and I had to get in together and fast.

Once I was done I came out and asked Nurse Jackie if she could give my client his medicine because I still was a little heated with him and I knew it was ungodly to be that way. Not even three minutes later Jackie was running out with water dripping from her hair that she had just gotten done before coming to work. All I could do was stand there with my hand over my mouth thinking if that was me he would be down in the basement on ice waiting to go get prepped for his homegoing service. It would have been a slow singing casket bringing day for him.

I ran over to help her clean herself off. We went to write a report upon him because something had to be done. The doctor finally came in to see him and informed us that he had seen him about a week ago and that he was diagnosed with a mental disorder. That is the moment I felt bad because I knew this man couldn't have been acting this way just to be mean. Here I was ready to let him meet his maker before his time.

The doctor prescribes him medicine to help him with some of the issues we were dealing with and for the rest of the day, we didn't have any more problems out of him. I pushed the earbud down in my ear a little bit more so that I could hear the music flowing. I need a spiritual touch right now because the devil was truly moving today. I got so wrapped up in my music until I was walking and swaying all at once. I had checked my last patient and decided I wanted to go back in to check on Mrs. Baker before going home.

"Hey sweetheart I know you are tired of seeing me today but I am about to go home and Juanita here will be taking over for me. Then you know I had to come back in and see my favorite patient of the day." I told her slightly pinching her big puffy cheeks.

Lula was a cocoa-colored big bone elderly lady; her hair was white as snow and had a few gray strings that looked almost silver. She looked as if she had just gotten her hair done but never combed out the curls. She put you in the mind of Gladys Knight, especially her cheeks.

"Come here sugar and give me a hug. You're a sweet little thang and don't you ever let anybody steal your joy. God wants to use you and the devil doesn't like it. He is going to come at you from all sides but you just stand and let the Lord fight that battle baby. Without God we can't make it in this world and as long as you live you always remember that." She told me and released me from the death grip she had around my neck.

I reached down and grabbed her hand to pray for her. *"Father God I thank you for letting Mrs. Lula and I cross paths today. She doesn't know it but she has been my inspiration today. I pray that you touch her body and heal her body in a mighty way. Lord, you are a miracle worker and there is no other God like you. You can do the unthinkable and Lord we are claiming healing over her feeble body, in Jesus name Amen.* I love you and it a thang you can do about it. I am sure you will be here tomorrow so I will see you in the morning. Juanita, you take care of this one right here." I told her as I left for the day.

On my way home I thought about the day I just had and couldn't wait to get home to take a nice hot bath and a much-needed nap. I was so lost in thought before I knew it I was home. I couldn't help but wonder if I had been speeding. I pulled into my driveway and made my way inside the house.

"Mommy hey you are home," Benny said almost knocking me down to give me a hug.

"Yes, I am. Let mommy go take a shower and get out these clothes." I replied as I made my way around to Ben laying a kiss on his lips before I replayed how my day went to him. Afterward, Benny sat back down on the floor to continue to watch TV, while Ben followed me to the room.

I went to my drawers to find me something comfortable to put on, while Ben went in and ran me a nice hot bubble bath. He turned the lights down and lit a few candles and placed them around the tub. I went in and was surprised because he hasn't done this in a while. I hugged him one last time before stripping down and stepping over into the water. An hour later after soaking and relaxing I stepped out of the tub, put on my clothes and join Bentley in my big king-sized bed. He massaged my back so good I was sleeping in no time at all.

Sharon

I was sitting in the choir stand when Bentley came in with his son Benny. This was the first time since they joined the church that I saw him at church without his wife. I didn't know if something had happened or not but I knew it had to be a good reason because she never let him get out of her eyesight. I know it must be a story behind that. The way Ben's eyes roam I could bet money I know what it has to do with.

Once he got Benny seated he made his way up to the front of the church and sat in his usual spot next to Pastor Elton. Before taking his seat, I was able to grab his attention long enough to wave my hand at him and he responded with a smile and nod of his head. That right there told me he could be as sly as a fox. He was trying not draw too much attention to him speaking.

Bentley came here a few years after me and out of all the other deacons, I could never get along with them like I do with Ben. They either are too old and set in their ways are they are my age and think they know it all. He was different he was funny, down to earth and easy to work with. I am sure that is what drew Glinda to him.

Nova is a pretty cool guy but he is nowhere as cool as he was when we first got together. We used to hang out like we were teenagers. Now he wants to be all serious about everything. When I am at home with him it is as if I don't even exist unless he is looking for something and can't find it himself. That gets dull, so that is the main reason I try to stay at the church helping Bentley as much as I do.

I so deep in my thoughts that choir director had to clear his throat several times to get my attention. I looked up and everyone was staring at me including Nova. He was looking as if I had embarrassed him or something. I slowly stood up and watched Derwin as he raised his hands and told us when to sing. He handed the microphone to Tameka to lead "Because of Who You Are." When we finished the song, the church had forgotten all about my daydreaming and was praising God to the fullest. People were running around the church while others were in tears. I must say Tameka sang that song today.

Pastor Elton said that Tameka had already led the spirit into the building so he would just go right into the sermon. Once everyone settled down and took their seats he instructed Bentley to start off with a prayer. Bentley prayed like he had sinned and fallen short of the glory and needed to repent. After he finished praying Pastor stood up and took the microphone.

"Good morning everybody," Is what he said while only half the church mumbled back to him.

'I said good morning everybody. Some of ya'll act like God didn't bless ya'll with the ability to open your mouth and speak today. Now I am trying this one more time, good morning church." Pastor Elton repeated.

"Good Morning" responded the members to the pastor sounding like one big loud choir all on one accord.

"Now that's more like it. All of you are sitting in here like you're dead. If you didn't come to praise the Lord you should have stayed at home. I don't know about you but I came here to get an overflow. I come to fill my cup with a spiritual blessing. I come to let my light shine so that others may see the God in me. Some of you can't get your praise on cause you to busy looking at your neighbor sitting beside or in front of you. While you are blocking your blessing sister so and so up there getting her's. Then you leave here and done missed yours because you can't wait to get home and get on the phone calling Mae Lee talking about chile did you see sister so and so in the church today, she must be going through with her husband again. That is where you are blocking your blessing again because she has given that problem with her husband over to the Lord for him to fight that battle. So, she gonna be alright, she got a right to praise him. The question is where is your husband and who he with. See I done started something let me hush before they are ready to put me out the church." Pastor

Elton preached to the congregation not caring if he stepped on anyone's toes or not.

He preached for a little while longer before he called Ben back up to close out the service with a prayer once more. Once Bentley was done everyone greeted each other with a friendly goodbye. I went down and thanked the pastor for an awesome word and before I could greet Bentley Nova tapped me on the shoulder and whispered him my ear, "let's go now" like he was aggravated. I looked back wave goodbye to Bentley, waved for my kids and walked out the church for Nova to drive us home.

The whole ride home was uncomfortable. You could feel the tension so thick it could be cut with a knife. I don't know what happened for him to be in such a bad mood before we left the house everything seemed to be fine. I didn't want to question him about anything because the children were in the car but I could tell that even they could feel something was wrong.

We pulled up in the yard and as soon as Nova stopped the kids jumped out of the car and ran toward the front door. I guess we were taking too long for the kids so Caleb ran back to the car and grabbed my house keys. As soon as Nova unhooked his seat belt I stopped him and asked him what was wrong with him.

"Nothing Sharon let's just go in the house." He responded but the look on his face was evident that he was lying.

"Look, Nova, I can look at you and tell that you have a problem so you may as well spit it out."

"What was your problem today Sharon you have been acting strange since the other day. The choir director had to clear his throat at least time times before you hear him. So please share what you had on your mind that had you so distracted." Nova said with a tone that let me know he was more than embarrassed he was angry.

"Nova you know I have been working on trying to get this business for the church off the ground, so when I got an idea that could help I think I drifted off into my own little world," I said hoping he would accept that answer and leave it alone.

The Deacon and His First Lady   Tammy T. Cross

"I tell you what whatever you got planned I hope it works out because you spend more time at the church and neglecting your family. Sometimes I feel you stay at the church just to be away from us." He commented right before swinging his seat beat off and proceeding toward the house.

"Now just wait one minute that is not fair Nova you know that is not true. You and the kids mean the world to me." I said trying not to break down in tears because I could see the kids peeking throw the window from inside the house.

"Can we talk about this later don't you see the kids staring out the blinds." He said trying to end the conversation.

"We will let it go for now but we will talk about it later and that's a promise." I spit out and turned around and stormed into the house.

I stormed into the house and straight to my room to get out of my church clothes. I walked back toward the front of the house and Nova was nowhere in sight. The kids were in their rooms doing whatever like they always do. I walked over and looked out the window and his car was still there. I then made my way to look out the back-patio window and he was sitting there like he was in a deep thought. I didn't bother him instead I went to the kitchen to see what we were going to have for dinner.

The way my mind was going I decided to just warm the leftover spareribs, bake beans and pasta salad we had the day before. Once everything was all done I had the kids clean their hands and I made their plates so when they were done they could go ahead and eat, I prepared Nova a plate and took it out to the patio along with an ice-cold Dr. Pepper. I wasn't hungry so I just got me a drink and sit down beside him and enjoyed the cool breeze.

"I waited a little while before I started a conversation. "Nova, do you really feel like I don't love you and the kids?" I asked him without looking in his direction.

"I didn't say you did not love us. I said I don't feel like you want to be around us. I think you use the church as a way of getting out of the house." He started to say before I cut him out.

"I get what you are saying honey but that is not the case. Pastor Elton came into the office the other day and told me I needed to go home to my family because I am always at the church work. Never thought I was neglecting my family. I just wanted to do something good for the church." Nova, I am sorry I never meant to put anything before my family." I stood up and walked around and sat in his lap to reassure him.

He looked at me and gave me a kiss that sent chills down the back of my spine. I grabbed his face and kissed him back forgetting that the kids were in the kitchen and could see us through the window. We were disturbed when Caleb brought his little behind out the door saying, "You to need to just get a room already," Causing Nova and me to laugh and Kara walking away as if we just made her lose her appetite.

"Caleb, just go back in the house and pull the blinds and you wouldn't have to worry about what is going on out here. By the way little boy, I just gave your dad a kiss that's all. I told him as I threw the towel that was on the table at him. Causing him to turn and run in the house.

I was so glad that day was over and I could get back to work at the church to clear my mind. I know Nova thinks that's an excuse to get away but to me, it's my stress reliever and I feel closer to God when I am working. "Hey, Sharon, you are here bright and early today. I am usually always here at least an hour before you." I heard Bentley say as he walked through the door behind me.

"Oh, good morning I was trying to get here bright and early just so that I could write down some ideas for the business. By the way, I got someone willing to donate us a bunch of coats that we could sale at a reasonable price and that could be a way to make a little money for the pastor's anniversary. I said standing up from his desk trying to move past him so that he could have his chair.

Upon moving passed him I tripped on the chair causing him to try and break my fall. I grabbed his arm to hold myself up and my face bumped him before we knew it my lips locked with his. I thought about what would happen if the pastor walked in and caught us. I pulled away quickly and excused myself to the bathroom for a few minutes.

I knew that what had just happened was wrong but at the moment it felt so right. I didn't know how I was going to come out and face Bentley or just how I would be able to look in Glinda's face knowing that I kissed her husband. I asked the Lord to forgive me checked my lip gloss and marched out the bathroom as if nothing ever happened.

I walked back to the office and sat at the desk and picked up the papers I had been going over before he came walking in. "So, what do you think about my idea with the coats? Do you think we could make enough to fund the program and give Pastor Elton a nice offering from us as members?" I asked trying to forget about the kiss.

"Sharon first thing first you do know before we move on with this work we need to address this issue we just had, right?" Ben asked me and I didn't feel the least bit worried about it. When I walked back in the room I was over it.

"What issue Ben?" I don't know what you are talking about. Besides, it was just a kiss that we stopped before it got out of hand. Just let it go so we can get back to work." I snapped because I felt he was making a big deal out of nothing.

He got up and shut the door so no one would walk up and hear our conversation. "Sharon, you do know that was wrong and that kiss should have never happened. You are married and so am I do you know how much trouble that could cause." He said nervously as if he has been caught up in a situation like this before.

I stood up and pulled him close to me, "you have to calm down like I said it was a small kiss. It was an accident Bentley I tripped and when our face hit it happened and there was no way of stopping it. Tell me you didn't enjoy it?' I moved closer and whispered in his ear and before moving away I leaned in kissing him once again.

Bentley went along with the kiss for a moment before he pulled away. Just as he walked back around to sit down Pastor Elton came walking in saying, "I thought I heard voices in here. What are you two working on now?"

"I was just telling Deacon Ben about this company that was willing to donate us a ton of coats. Being that winter is right around the corner and the church anniversary is coming up, this could be a good way for us to raise some money. I thought some of the parents that can't really afford to buy a nice warm coat could buy it from us for a low price. It will help them save money and give us money to put on the anniversary program." I took over the conversation since Ben was at lost for words.

"Is this so Deacon, I tell you Sharon always seem to come through for The House of Repentance C.O.G.I.C all the time." Pastor Elton said as he came around and hugged my neck.

"Yes, Pastor she came up with that idea all on her own and I must say it is a great idea," Bentley said now looking calmer than before.

"I am going to get out of here and let you two get back to work. I have some work of my own to finish down in my office," the pastor said right before he turned to leave.

Bentley stood up and said," Pastor I believe I am going to leave early today, I am not feeling so well and I don't want to get no one else sick." Looking back from the pastor and then to me.

Pastor Elton nodded his head and exited the room. Ben waiting until he heard the door to the pastor's office close before he said a word. "If he would have walked in on us that could have caused a lot of trouble you do know that don't you."

"It didn't so just calm down and you aren't sick why are you leaving?" I asked him.

"I got too much to lose and if I stay here that is exactly what will happen." He said grabbing his keys off the desk leaving me standing in his office like a love-sick puppy.

Since Bentley left early I guess I will go home and surprise my husband with dinner. I walked down to the pastor's office and let him know since we had a plan set up I was going to go home early if he didn't need me to do anything else.

"Sharon, you go on home I am going to be fine here. I got a few things I need to work on and I will be going home soon also."

I pulled his door close and walked out to my car and drove home. I wanted to show Nova that I did love him so I fixed his favorite dinner. I cooked him a nice juicy T-bone steak, baked potato with butter, sour cream and cheese on top. I also made him a chef salad to go along with it. The kids came home before Nova and were excited to see me already at home. I had them to go do their homework so that when Nova came home we could all eat together as a family.

An hour later Nova came through the door looking like he had just had a hard day at work. I wanted him to come in and put his belongings down before I moved in to greet him with a kiss. He walked into the kitchen and over to the stove and the smile that spread across his face made me feel so good.

"So, I take it you are happy with your meal," I asked already knowing what he would say.

"Happy isn't the word, man do you know how long I waited for you to make this. I could just do a praise dance right here in the middle of the kitchen floor." Nova said all at the same time doing a dance that looked like the running man. The dance we use to think was so cool back in the days.

The kids were at the table laughing so hard they almost fell out of their chairs. I had to bust up the party so we could eat before the food got cold. When we were all done eating and the kitchen was clean we all laid around like a bunch of stuffed piglets.

Bentley

The next morning, I woke up and my wife was not in bed. I could hear her in the bathroom so I used the front bathroom to myself wash up. I then went into the kitchen and fixed her a breakfast sandwich and a cup of coffee to go. She walked out just as I finished making her breakfast. I kissed her goodbye, walked her out the door and watched as she drove off down the road.

When I turned around Benny was at the table eating his favorite cereal "Captain Crunch." "Good morning son, I need you to hurry and eat so we can get dressed for church. Mommy had to work so she won't be going with us today." I told him as I saw the look of disappointment form on his face.

"Why does she have to work today? She never has to work on Sunday." Benny asked sounding like he wanted to cry.

"Clean your face up; you are too big to be whining like that. Now when you are done cleanly that bowl out and get your clothes off the ironing board and get dressed." I scolded him because sometimes be can sound like a real baby.

"Yes Sir," he replied and made his way to the kitchen to clean his cereal bowl.

By the time I came out of the room, he was dressed and ready for church. I got my keys and my wallet placing it in my back pocket, we hopped in the car and drove to the church. The parking lot was already packed. I pulled in to the first parking spot I saw and led Benny in, got him seated before I took my seat

It was odd going to church without my wife because normally she was off and able to join us. The moment I walked in the church I could tell that Sharon had something on her mind by the way she was staring at me. What I didn't know was if it had to do with work or me. I didn't play much into it, instead, I brushed it off and join in with the service.

The Deacon and His First Lady — Tammy T. Cross

When the choir stood up to sing, once they got Sharon's attention they sang the roof off the church. Man, the spirit was in the building so strong I couldn't hold myself in my seat. When the pastor called my name for me to pray I didn't hear him until he tapped me on my shoulder. Even then I could hardly pray for praising God. I said a quick prayer and handed the microphone back over to him.

After he got up he brought the congregation to their feet with that powerful sermon he preached. The only ones that were sitting down were the ones that felt like he was picking on them and they were the usual messy petty Betty's. Anybody with sense would have been blessed with a message that powerful.

Church was over and Nova pushed Sharon out the church so fast I didn't even get to go over to shake his hand. Benny was sad because he couldn't chat with Caleb much. I went over to Benny and told him they may have been in a hurry and that he would be able to talk with him another time. I knew deep down they had something else going on by the mean look Nova had on his face when the choir director couldn't get his wife's attention.

Benny and I left the church and decided to stop at Bushes Chicken to grab us a bite to eat. We went inside to eat, once we were done we went home and sat down and watched television. A few hours later we heard the door unlock and Glinda came walking in. Benny was happy to see her and ran to give her a hug.

I looked at my wife and saw that she was tired, so I told my son to step back and let her go get cleaned up. I noticed her looking for clothes and decided it would be nice to run her a nice warm bubble bath. She always had a few candles on the side of the tub, so I took it upon myself to light them so that she could relax while taking her bath. I went to the room to join her in the comfort of our bed when she was all done.

After her bath, I massaged her back until she was asleep. She must have been tired because she didn't wake up until the next morning. I got up and went to play the game with Benny until bedtime. I made sure Benny had his bath before I went to join my wife in bed. I couldn't fall asleep at first so I laid there and watched my wife sleeping peacefully until I had fallen asleep myself.

    The next morning Benny headed to school, Glinda went to work and I went over to the church to see what I could get done. I walked into the office and Sharon was already there. I went in and started talking to her and she interrupted the conversation by making a pass at me. I didn't know what had hit me when she planted a kiss on me as I was trying to break her fall. I guessed she knew that what she did was wrong because she had to leave out of the room to get herself together.

    At least I thought she had learned her lesson until she tried me again and this time we were almost caught by the pastor. I must admit at one point in time I couldn't resist her soft lips and kissed her back until I had a flashback of the beat down William put on me years ago. Once Pastor Elton came walking in on us I knew it was time to go or there would be a ton of trouble.

    I don't know what Sharon was thinking. I can't let her get me caught up like this again. The main reason Glinda and I moved here is to start our lives over. I cause so many problems back in our old hometown, that I'm too embarrassed to go back and visit some of my old friends. I also didn't want to take the chance of running into Gracie an old fling.

    I was so into my thoughts of what happened down at the church I almost missed my exit that led to my house. I threw my signal light on and sped up to switch lanes to make the turn. After making two lights and three right turns I was sitting in my front yard. I sat in my car for a minute trying to get myself together before I went inside the house.

    I made my way out of the car ten minutes later and up the walkway that led to the front door. I found the key to unlock the door and slowly walked inside. I was happy to find Glinda was still at work. That gave me some time to think about everything that had just happened with Sharon. I knew if Glinda finds out about this there will be trouble in the palace tonight.

    I didn't have much to do at home so I went outside in the backyard and grilled up a few burgers so that when my wife comes home she could relax without cooking. The moment I took the meat off the grill I walked back into the kitchen to find my wife walking through the door. She was looking like she had just lost her best friend.

"Babe, are you alright?" I asked looking at her red eyes noticing that she had been crying.

"No, I am not. The lady Mrs. Baker that I was telling you about yesterday passed away today. I don't understand what happened one minute she was in good spirit and telling me about God and the next minute she was gone. I went to go let her know that I was leaving for the day and talk to her a bit before my release nurse came. As soon as I walked in I noticed she didn't move and when I went over to her bed I touched her arm to see if she had a pulse and she was gone. She had a DNR so there was nothing we could do to save her." Glinda said as she fell over into my arms and cried like a newborn baby.

I had to lead her over to the couch because she was a tab bit bigger than me and my little boney self-holding her up wasn't happening. I sit there and let her cry it out and waited for her to tell me more about what happened. When I saw that she wasn't crying any longer I was able to ask her a question.

"Glinda what exactly was her reason for being in the hospital in the first place. I mean I know you told me but we talk about all your patients I need a little refresher." I told her giving her my undivided attention.

"The poor old lady came in with a broken hip. She had a spirit that was so lovely and strong you could feel it when you walked through her room door. She was completely fine and the next minute she wasn't. I know they say God doesn't make mistakes but I don't understand how someone could take a turn for the worst so fast." Glinda managed to mumble out before she went into another crying spell.

I looked at the clock and noticed it was almost time for our son to come home. I told her to go clean up and go relax in our room for a while because I didn't want Benny to come and see her all upset. One thing about Benny is he is very protective of Glinda and will go into defense mode in a minute.

I went back and finished up dinner. Benny came strolling in hungry as a horse. Once he put down his book bag and washed up he was at the table before anyone had to tell him what to do. "Well good afternoon to you young man. You must be starving because you didn't say one word when you walked in and then went straight to the table."

"Good afternoon dad and yes I didn't eat lunch today because I didn't know they were having that nasty imitation fish and I didn't bring my own lunch." He said as he stood up to move around the table to dab my hand before hugging me. This is the way he and I have greeted each other for years.

"Man, why didn't you call me. I would have brought you a lunch to the school?" I turned and asked him before he took his seat back at the table.

"Dad I knew you had to work and I didn't want to bother mom," he replied.

I was just about to tell him never feel like he is bothering me when he blurted out, "Speaking of mom I saw her car in the garage where is she?"

"Uh, your mom had a long day at work sh…." I attempted to say before she walked in the room answering Benny's question. I just turned and went back to the kitchen to fix their plates.

"Hey Benny baby, I was taking a little nap I had a long day at work but nothing you should worry about. Did I hear you say you missed lunch today?" Glinda asked Benny sounding upset because he missed lunch.

"Yes, ma'am but don't worry I had a bag of chips in my bag to hold me until I got home." He looked at her with his big puppy dog eyes and said trying not to make her feel bad.

I tell you the two of them are like putty in each other's hands. I just shook my head and walked into the kitchen and returned with their plates. I then went back to get mine along with an ice-cold pitcher of lemonade. We sat down and ate as Benny ran down his whole day to his mom and me, as we laughed at the silly jokes that he threw in from time to time.

    After dinner was over Benny and Glinda cleaned the kitchen and then sat down at the table to go play a card game. I went to my room and sat down at the desk and read my bible for a while. Once I was done I tried to come up with some ideas that we could do that could also raise money for our church. My mind was going so crazy about the shenanigans that Sharon tried to pull I couldn't get any work done at all. I leaned back in my chair and place both of my hands behind my back. I thought and thought for a moment before I came to the conclusion that it's best not to tell Glinda about what happened. After all, it was Sharon that made the pass.

Glinda

Man, I really didn't feel like going to work today because I was still hurt from the last of Mrs. Baker. I asked my supervisor could I work with the babies for a while because I didn't want to be anywhere near the room she was in. My supervisor understood and agreed to let me work with the babies. I was excited about that because I really enjoyed spoiling those adorable newborn babies.

Later I ran into Jackie in the hall and she looked as if she was having a bad day. "Hey, Jackie are you doing ok? You look like your day is not going so well." I walked up and asked her as I gave her a hug.

"Girl that ole coot that we got down in the room with the mental problem. You know exactly who I am talking about. He won't take his meds today and he got me wanting to pull out all of my hair." Jackie responded as she rubbed her had through the thin short bob she wore.

Jackie is a very sweet nurse, she is about five feet tall even and weighed every bit of one hundred and sixty pounds. Her skin was so light she could pass as an albino. She had gray eyes and her short thin bob was a honey blond. Looking at her you would think she was white but she was all black.

"Don't tell me Mr. Pillar is at it again. Why don't they just send him up on the fifth floor where they are more skilled to work with a patient like him?" I asked trying to figure out what was taking them so long to see that fool was in the wrong part of the hospital. Even Stevie Wonder could see that foolery.

"His family is against it they say he is perfectly fine and is just being mean," Jackie said as she gave me the side eye. I hated when she did it because it made her look cockeyed and her eye is jumping like she was really an albino. I think she is one because she has all the signs, but she swears that she is not.

"They all must be coo coo for cocoa puffs then if they can't see he has a few loose screws," I responded and twirled my finger around making a crazy move that looked like I was talking in sign language.

"Girl there has to be something wrong with them but I tell you what, if he throws one more object at me he is gonna come up missing," Jackie said before she turned around to leave. I stood there and laughed so hard at the way she rolled her little stubby neck before walking away.

I went back to the nursery and fed the last baby before I went home. I tell you this baby was so beautiful it made me want another child. She looked as if she could be a little cabbage patch doll. She was a little white baby with cheeks the color of a beautiful peach colored rose. Her eyes were as blue as the ocean and her hair was blonde. She was born 8 1/2 pounds and 4oz. She was a big baby and when you held her it felt as if you were holding a brick she was so solid.

I went over my notes with Lisa the incoming nurse after laying the baby back in her crib. I walked down to the nurse station to meet up with Jackie so we could walk out to the car garage together and talk about how the remainder of her day went. "You ready to go Jackie? Lord knows I am ready to go. I have heard enough baby cries for today." I grabbed my purse out of my locker and told Jackie.

"Yes, I am ready because if I have to go back in that room one more time I swear I will be unemployed. They need to seriously do something with that man." Jackie said to me and I felt bad because I was so emotional about Mrs. Baker that I couldn't stand to be on that floor. I guess tomorrow I will suck it up and go back to give her a break.

"Jackie, I am sorry. I will ask my supervisor can I come back to give you a little break."

"You would do that for me Glinda?" Jackie asked as she rushed to me almost knocking me down with a hug.

"Wayment now you almost knocked me down with all of that stuff you are packing back there girl. You got to be easy with a girl like me you know I am delicate." I told her as we both burst out into laughter.

"Come on here girl and let's get out of this hospital before we get put out for being so loud," Jackie said as she pushed me out the door.

On our way out, we ran into my friend Kita that has been working the night shift lately. I stopped her and gave her the biggest hug." Kita, I haven't seen you in a while, how have you been?" I asked her almost in tears because I was happy to see her.

"Hey Glinda, don't start the waterworks now with your sensitive behind. You know we are all crybabies, we can't stand all that crying. Ain't that right Jackie," Kita asked her pulling her in for a hug.

"Who are you telling, she got me crying and just a few minutes ago I was ready to commit a murder," Jackie whispered so no one would take her seriously and try to report her.

"Girl, who are you trying to kill?" Kita whispered back at Jackie.

"That mental fool down there," Jackie responded pointing in the direction of Mr. Pillar's room.

We all started to laugh and Kita hugged us again and left before she was late for work. Jackie and I chatted all the way to our cars. I hugged her with one last goodbye and we went our own ways. I jumped on HWY 6 and drove all the way home in complete silence. Pulling up at home I noticed that Benny and Bentley were both already home and playing catch the football in the yard.

"There is my little Prescott and Romo." I joked as I got out of the car walking toward the both of them.

"Hey mommy," Benny yelled as he ran toward me giving me a huge bear hug.

"Hold on Ben you can't be so rough with your mom. Boy, you are getting too big to be rushing up on her like that, I have told you before. I know you love your mom and all but if she falls down I am going to be angry with you." Bentley fussed at Benny.

"It's okay to hug me but not so hard baby but anyways how was your day at school?" Glinda asked as she walked into the house, looking at her husband as if he was too hard on Ben for trying to protect her from falling.

I guess the boys have had enough of playing catch because when I went in the house they were right on my heels. After I got all cleaned up we sat at the table and played a game of Uno and had a wonderful time.

"Mommy I have beat you and dad so much that I am tired of playing. I am going to my room and let you and dad play while I go play my game." Benny said as he threw down his cards leaving Ben and me sitting at the table looking crazy.

We decided that we had played enough Uno ourselves so we put down the cards and started to talk. I told him all about how the old man at the hospital has been giving us all a hard time. We talked so much our mouths were dry as cotton. Ben walked to the kitchen and poured us a glass of his freshly squeezed lemonade. I tell you it was so good it gave me life the moment it hit my taste buds.

"How is the project going down at the church?" I as Bentley as I took a gulp of my lemonade before setting it down on the coffee table that was sitting in the middle of the floor in front of us.

"It's been going well. We have to start making some sales before we can really know how well we are going to do. I have to meet with Sharon later to see what day we plan to do our first coat sale." Ben responded by drinking his lemonade so fast, that you would have sworn he had something spicy in his mouth and he was trying to cool his mouth down.

"Are you ok Ben? You look as if something is bothering you." I asked him noticing the way he started to wiggle around in his seat when I mention the project he was working on at the church. He started to make me feel a little uneasy about him working with Sharon but I told him I would trust him so I am going to do just that.

"I am fine Glinda, Just a little thirsty that's all. You know this lemonade is the bomb and it is really hitting the spot right now. He said as he sat the glass on the table beside mine doing a dance. To show me just how much he was enjoying his drink.

"Come on honey it is not that good." I joked and we both began to laugh as he softly hit me with the plush pillow that was sitting on the end of the sofa we were sitting on in the middle of the living room.

After our talk, Ben went to the bathroom leaving his cellphone on the coffee table. He had it turned upside down so when it rung I couldn't see who was calling him. I started to pick it up and see who was calling but if I was going to trust him I have to prove to myself as well as him that I could do it. A few minutes later it started to buzz again and before I could put my hand on it to answer I yanked it back like I had touched a hot stove and got up to leave out of the room.

When he came back in the room I walked back and sit down beside him on the couch beside. "Your phone was ringing honey," I told him trying to see if he was going to pick it up and return the call.

"Did you check to see who it was Glinda?" He asked knowing that I never answer his phone. Deep down inside I think he was hoping that I didn't answer.

"Now you know I never answer your phone, Ben," I told him giving him the side eye.

A few minutes later he picked up the phone and started messing with the buttons. I was sitting on one end of the couch and he was sitting on the other end, so I couldn't really tell what he was doing. I tried to hide the fact that I was getting upset because I am starting to see signs of his past surfacing again, but it was hard. I got up and walked to my room and left him in the living room playing on his phone.

A few minutes later he came walking, "Hey Glen, I have to run down to the church for a minute I will be back in a little while." Ben said as he walked upon me giving me a kiss on the cheek before walking out the door.

Sharon

"Pastor Elton I am going to be doing some work in the office down the hall. Is there something you need me to do before I get started?" I asked him as I stood in the door of his office.

"When you get done with what you are doing can go over this finance sheet to see if everything looks right to you.?" He asked me handing me the folder he was sitting at his desk looking over.

"Pastor I can do it right now since I have to wait for Bentley to get here. It won't take me but a few minutes to do this anyways." I responded as I took the folder out of his hand and headed back to the small office at the other end of the hall.

Before I could get to the other end of the hall Pastor Elton yelled out. "Take your time I am about to leave you can return them to me tomorrow."

I yelled backed, "Yes Sir" and walked on down the hall to the office.

I was just about done with the church's finance report when Bentley came walking in. I looked up at him and gave him a smile. I didn't say anything to him I just slid him the paper that I had made up with the events had I planned for us, while I finished the report for Pastor Elton.

"I will be right back Bentley I have to go return this folder back to the Pastor before he leaves," I told him as I stood up to walk out of the office.

"Looks like you won't be giving that to him today because I just pasted him up walking out of the door," Bentley told me and it made me feel all happy inside because now we were there alone.

"Oh well let me go and place this on his desk so when he comes in tomorrow he can get it," I told him because I had to go see for myself that we were really there alone.

The Deacon and His First Lady — Tammy T. Cross

I don't know why Ben is playing so hard to get. I know Glinda can't be keeping him all that happy. I know he wants me but he is scared to make a move. I can tell by the way he looks at me when I am in his presence. Today I am going to see just how much he wants me if I got to make the first move again.

I walked around the church to make sure the pastor was really gone before I returned to the office. When I returned he was sitting at the desk looking all good and smelling so good I could have sopped him up with a biscuit. I walked up behind him as I shut the door to the office and began to massage the back of his neck.

He kept reading over the plans as he rolled his neck like the message felt so good. I moved from his neck down to his shoulders and the look he had on his face was the look of an angel floating around in heaven. Once I had him in a zone I kissed the tip of his ear making my way down to his neck. When he didn't move let's just say heaven was made right in that little office.

After I had completed my mission I went to the bathroom, fixed my clothes, makeup, and hair and went back to the office to talk about the upcoming events. When I made it back to the office he was sitting there with his elbows on his knees, the palm of his hands held his face and he was bent over sitting in the chair as if he was praying for forgiveness.

I eased back in acting like I was sorry for what had happened. Knowing good and well I wanted him as much as he wanted me. Come on Nova isn't doing much for me so I know Glinda can't be handling up on her end because he wouldn't have just let me have it like we were newlyweds on a honeymoon.

I started a conversation out of the blue, "What do you think about how I planned out the events. I thought maybe the first event could be us setting up in the church parking lot and sell the coats on Saturday. We can post a status on the church Facebook website to let everyone know about it right now if you agree."

"Sharon how can you talk about an event after what just happened. I don't want to get caught up like this. You know we

The Deacon and His First Lady   Tammy T. Cross

both are married. How could you do me like this?" He asked me as if he didn't just lay me out flat on this desk after a kiss on his neck.

"What do you mean how could I do this to you. You act like you didn't have a part in this. I know a kissed didn't make you do what you did. You could have said no." I fussed at him as he tried to make it seem like it was me and only me.

"You do this stuff to me every time you are in my presence. We can't be doing this like I told you before." He replied tried to convince me he was serious.

I stood up and walked around the desk stood in his face and placed both of his hands on my thighs. "So, mean to tell me you don't want all of this."

He was sitting in the chair looking me up and down like a dog drooling at a big juicy bone. I moved his hand after standing there for several minutes without him saying a word. I grabbed my purse and strutted out of the office looking over my shoulder at him look like a lovesick puppy.

When I got outside I tried to start my car and it wouldn't make a sound. I hit the steering wheel and thought maybe God is punishing me for messing around with Ben. I fought with it for about ten minutes before I came walking out of the church.

He pretended as if he didn't see me but (we) he noticed that my car wouldn't start he stopped in his tracks turned around and came back and tried to help. Once we couldn't get it started he offered to give me a ride home. I grabbed my purse from the passenger seat of my car and hopped into Bentley's truck and he drove me home.

Once we got there I noticed he was looking around for something to clean the oil off his hands. He had gotten them all dirty trying to fix my car. I offered him to get out and go inside to wash his hands before he left. At first, he refused and but he finally agreed.

When we got there my kids were at a friend's house and Nova was still working. I showed him where the hall bathroom was and went to my room to get comfortable. I hurried to get back out before he left. When I came out and he saw me standing there in nothing but a robe, he couldn't do anything but stare at me.

I walked over to him and placed his hands around my waist and I landed a kiss on him so strong he almost fell over. "Sharon what are you doing? Nova the kids can walk in and catch us. I told you we can't." Before he could finish his sentence, I hit him with another kiss. A while later we both had driven down the road to glory for the second time today.

This time instead of me rushing to the bathroom it was Bentley. He went to go and clean up before he goes home to Glinda and his son. I laid back on the couch and laughed to myself knowing this man was weak for me. I jumped up when he came out and walked him to the door. He walked out without saying goodbye but I wasn't bothered at all.

After he left I went cleaned up myself before the kids and Nova came home. I didn't have the strength to cook thanks to Bentley so I ordered Pizza Hut. Just as I expected they were starving when they came running through the door. Nova wasn't too big for Pizza so I played the good wife and ordered him his favorite hot wings.

"Hey everyone, I see you guys are eating pizza tonight. Your mom must have had a long day down at the church too." Nova said as he walked in kissed me and hugged both kids before putting his belongings down.

"I ordered you your favorite wings and to answer your question, yes I had a long day. We came up with an idea to do a coat sale on Saturday. Once we see how that works that will give us an idea of how the next event may go." I told Nova as I brought him a cold drink and his food to the couch where he was now sitting.

"That is great I know Pastor Elton will be happy," he replied.
Bentley
I drove home thinking about what had just transpired between Sharon and me. I was praying when I got home Glinda wouldn't read me and know that something wasn't right. I made it home a little quicker than I wanted to. I guess Glinda was tired

because when I came home she was fast asleep. I tipped in and grabbed some clothes and took a shower without waking her.

That shower gave me life, it felt so good I forgot all about waking Glinda with all the noise I was making. I walked out of the bathroom and she was still asleep. I eased back out of the room and peeked in on Benny. He was so busy playing his game he didn't even notice I was standing in his doorway.

I went into the kitchen and grabbed me a glass of lemonade but in my mind, I wish it was a bottle of wine. The way my mind was going I needed something strong to slow it down. Too bad when I became a deacon I gave all the drinking up. Being around Sharon is definitely going to make me start drinking all over again. I know I am just as wrong as her but she really knows how to get next to me.

I laid down on the couch and started watching the western movie "Gunsmoke" and before long it was watching me. Soon after I got into a good sleep and Glinda was waking me up, telling me to come get in bed. I sat up to clear my head and she helped me get up to go to the bedroom.

The next morning when I woke up Benny was already gone to school, and Glinda was gone to work. I felt like I had dodged a bullet. Now I have time to get a story together before she comes home. I know by the way she was acting when I left last night she had something on her mind. Then when I kissed her she didn't return one back to me like she normally does.

I tried to stick around the house to stay away from Sharon because if things keep going the way we both are bound to get caught. I went to the dining room to read my bible to try to start over with God because of the sin I committed with Sharon. A few minutes later I pushed the bible aside and started to think about the way I had Sharon embraced in my arms and how mesmerized she had me when she kissed the tips of my earlobes. Just the grip that I had on the bible loosen up and the bible hit the desk scaring me half to death. I said out loud, "Lord I hear you and I am sorry."

I picked my bible back up and began to read again and just like before I drifted off into my thoughts again. I could imagine her walking out in that leopard printed short robe half open showing nothing but her morning glory. When that woman walked upon me and caressed my inner thigh, I turned in to a loose cannon that blew her to pieces. While I was starting a fire with Sharon, Glinda was the last thing on my mind and now I am sitting here feeling sorry for myself. When I should be thinking how Glinda would feel if she got wind of all this madness.

  I got tired of sitting in the house so I thought I would go to the store and pick up a few items we needed for the house. I threw on a pair of black and gray jogging pants with a grey t-shirt that had black sleeves. I then sat down on the side of the bed and slide on my black Nike socks I pulled out of my sock drawer that sets on the side of my bed. Once I got them on I reached by the side of my bed and slipped my feet in my all black Nikes. When I finished up I jumped in my truck and drove down to Wal-Mart.

  Moments later I was pulling in the parking lot, parking in the nearest spot available. I put the list that Glinda had placed on the frig in my pocket. I hurried up and jogged across the parking lot to get out of the way of the cars that was leaving and coming. I was standing in the aisle reading the list to see which one Glinda needed when suddenly, I felt a tap on my shoulder.

  "So, I guess you are following me now," I heard a voice saying to me before I could even turn around.

  "Nah, just picking up a few items my wife needed for the house," I replied trying to sound like I didn't have time for a conversation.

  The look Sharon gave me when I said the words my wife let me know that she had a problem with Glinda, that only she knew about." Your wife huh! Well, you didn't seem like you had a wife when you were all cuddled up with me." Sharon spits out as if she wasn't married herself.

  "Yes, wife now don't act like you don't know Glinda and I are married. You started all of this mess and I didn't want anything to do with it."

"Could have fooled me, Ben. I couldn't tell you didn't want me by the way you tore into me like a predator looking for a victim to prey on." She said trying to make it seemed if I touched her first.

"I am the prey because if I am not mistaken you put those long acrylic claws on me," I yelled removing her hand off my shoulder that was still sitting there since she tapped me.

"Hey, Ben is everything alright." I heard another voice say coming from behind me once again.

"I-I am fine. I was just having a conversation with Sharon," I responded looking as if I had been caught red-handed cheating.

"Just checking, I thought I heard you yelling and I was trying to make sure you weren't having any problems." Kita, Glinda's friend said as she was standing there with her hand on her right hip, looking like she wanted to drop kick, Sharon.

"Ben why is she standing here mugging me looking like a stuffed bell pepper? Sharon blurted out and I knew that Wal-Mart was about to be rearranged by the looked Kita gave her as she placed her purse in her basket and pushed it to the side.

"A stuffed bell pepper? Lil girl you got me all messed up. You know what? I am not going to stoop to your level and have me repenting. Oh, and by the way, if you ever step to me like that again, I am going to break you down to the lowest denominator." Kita snatched her purse out the basket, turned and walked away leaving the basket sitting in the middle of the aisle. Sharon was just about to say something when suddenly Kita was headed toward us.

"Bentley are you sure you are alright? I thought I heard you two arguing." Kita asked looking at me trying to block Sharon out like she was a ghost or something.

"I am good Kita we are working on a project together for the church and we had a disagreement about something that's all," I told her trying to sound convincing.

"Long as you are good I am going to keep it moving," she said grabbing her basket she left the first time she walked off while rolling her eyes as she walked away.

Sharon was about to say something again when I gave her a look to warn her not to say nothing. At this moment I was so ticked off that I left my basket sitting there right along with Sharon and walked out of the store. I jumped in my truck drove over to Family Dollars grabbed everything on the list and went home.

I was so mad that I threw my phone in the seat of the truck after I came out of Wal-Mart. So, when I made it home and put everything away I checked my phone and I swear I had missed about twenty calls from Sharon. I didn't want Glinda to come home and she still blowing me up so I sat down at the kitchen table and called her back.

"Why are haven't you been answering the phone, Ben?" Sharon said in a tone as if nothing had just happened at the store. She wasn't even thinking about this mess getting back to my wife.

"Man, Sharon you be tripping. You can't be running up on me like that in public. Man, if Glinda gets word of this she is going to kill the both of us," I told her.

"I am sorry Ben I didn't mean to cause any trouble I just couldn't stand to see that woman all up in your face like she knows so much about you," she replied.

"That woman happens to be my wife's best friend Kita and if word gets back to her we were standing in the middle of the store arguing. She not gonna take that to well. She will be the one to round you up and break you down to the lowest denominator."

"I don't want any problems with anyone but that ain't why I called you. Can you come over to my house tomorrow morning? I have something I want you to look over to see if you think it may help the church raise some money." Sharon said and by the tone of her voice I could tell she seemed sincere, so I agreed and hung up the phone.

Glinda

Another Sunday is here and it is time for my family and me to go to the house of the lord, one more time. We look forward to getting our cups filled with a spiritual potion from the Lord. Although I noticed my husband was dragging his feet this morning. I also happen to notice that he hasn't been running down to the church as much as he uses to. That is unlike him because he loves being at the church more than life itself.

"Babe, what's bothering you? You seem a bit sluggish today." I looked at him and asked as he sat on the bed and held his church socks in his hand. Like God's house is the last place he wanted to be this morning.

"It's nothing Glinda, I am just nervous about this coat sale, we have coming up next Saturday. I had my mind dead set on it this past weekend but due to the rain, we had to cancel it. I want the Pastor's anniversary to be a big success. If we don't make the amount of money we need we may have to cut down on some of the things we planned on doing for him." Bentley sat back on the bed and responded to me.

"Well, that's the more reason you need to be down at the church. There are plenty things you guys can do to raise money. You and Sharon can get the youth kids together and do a car wash or bake sale. I think that will make a nice piece of change. When I was a kid my mother used to do it with all of the kids at my old church." I said as I pranced around the room trying to figure out what pair of shoes I wanted to wear.

Ben still had a strange look on his face and I was beginning to think his problem was much bigger than the church anniversary, but I didn't say another word and proceeded to get dressed. Since the weather was starting to cool down I decided to slip on my black wedged heels with the gold bow on top. They matched my outfit perfectly.

When I was done getting dressed I went to Benny's room to see if he was dressed and ready to go. When I got to the door he had his church clothes on, his bible sitting on his bed and was playing his game like always. "Come on young man it's time to go and get our praise on." I went in and handed him his Bible, while he turned his game off and followed me out of the room.

"Bentley are you ready yet? If you keep poking around in there you are going to have us late. I fussed as he comes marching out of the room.

"I AM COMING, hold your horses, Glinda I was trying to make sure I had everything." He snapped at me and I almost broke my neck swinging it back to look at him. I don't know who he thought I was but he will get his wig split in half if he snaps at me one more time.

"Benny, baby here goes the keys go on to the car we will be there in a minute. Bentley one thing I know and two things for sure if you ever holler at me like that again I am going to owe God a ton of I owe you. I will be forced to set the holy ghost to the side and let Satan have a few seconds of fame." I strolled up to him and looked him straight in the eye so he could understand every word I said.

"I am sorry honey I didn't mean to sound so mean. I am still a little frustrated and I kinda took it out on you. My bad it won't happen again," he replied trying to walk past me heading for the door.

"No sir I am not done with you. What is really the problem Ben? Does it have anything to do with the argument you and Sharon were having in the middle of Walmart a few days ago? I hadn't mentioned it because I thought that you would tell me about it. Yes, Nakita told me all about how she almost mopped the floor with her. Do you mind telling me what that was all about?

"Uhmmm yeah well Sharon and I couldn't agree on one of the events. So, when she ran into me at Walmart she asked me had I decided on what I wanted to do yet. I told her I was out picking up supplies for you and that right now wasn't the time to discuss the church in the middle of the store and she got offended." He told me, sounding like he was shaking in his pants.

"I agree with you, leave that mess at the church honey. Sharon is my girl and all but Kita is to, and I hope she doesn't step to her like that again because if she does Kita may have her place in a body bag. I myself ain't taking any part in any of this. Come on Ben let's go before Pastor Elton think we are MIA." I waved for him to move a little faster out the door so we could drive over to the church.

As we were walking out the door Benny was on his way back in to see what was taking us so long. "We are coming boy go get back in the car." I fussed at him as he ran and hopped in the back seat and buckled up so fast, all I could do was laugh."

We drove down to the church and hurried in because we could hear the harmony from the choir coming from behind the church walls and floating all the way out to the parking lot. I saw Ben shifting his tie back and forward like it was choking him. By the time I was about to ask him if he was ok he moved his hand from his tie and walked into the church and found his seat in the pulpit right next to Pastor Elton's seat.

Benny went and sit next to Caleb and Trey and I sit beside Kita who happened to be off today. I was glad about that because I was missing her presence in the church. Sitting down beside her I saw that Kita and Sharon were eyeing each other. I tapped Kita on the leg and softly told her to behave. She turned and looked at me and we smile before we tuned in to the pastor that was now getting up to speak.

"Good morning church today we are going to talk about holding grudges. Some of you are walking in the church expecting a word from the lord, but you can't let go a grudge you have with your brother or sister in Christ. God isn't blessing anyone that can't show someone that is in your circle or was once in your circle love. Walking around mumbling chile I use to be friends with her until she rubbed me the wrong way but now honey I don't deal with her anymore. Then you expect God to forgive you. What makes you better than the one that rubbed you the wrong way." Pastor Elton preaches and looked in Kita and Sharon direction as if he knew about the mess that they had going on.

"Amen," shout the congregation.

"You are walking around after church is over shaking hands with the other members and when sister so in so come in your direction you got your nose all turn up like you smell dog poo or something. People Y'all better let go of the grudges before the same grudges you are holding on to have you sitting at the head of Satan's table. I will not teach on that long today but the holy spirit dropped that on me." He said, and I could tell it made Kita and Sharon feel some type of way by the looks on their faces.

"Preach preacher," shouted the elderly ladies that sat on the front row of the church every Sunday.

He preached on the subject for about thirty more minutes before he handed the floor over to the ushers. They marched to the front and instructed the member to stand and bring their offering starting from the rear. Each member walked around and dropped their money in the basket that sat in the middle of the wood table that read "Do in Remembrance of Me," as the choir sang a hymn.

Once everyone was seated Ben stood up and blessed the offering. He then handed back over to the pastor so he could dismiss us from the service. When he was all done we walked around and greeted one another like we always did before going home.

Ben and I stood in the middle of our bedroom talking about how Pastor Elton preached his sermon today. "I tell you the Pastor read Kita and Sharon today, didn't he?" I laughed and asked Bentley.

"Why you figure he was directing his message toward them?" I turned and looked at Bentley like he had not just sat in the same services as I was. I can't believe he asked a dumb question like that.

"What church where you at today Ben? Everybody in the church knew who he was talking about. The tension the two of them have for each other is so thick. That when they are in each other's presences it could be cut with a knife."

"Oh yeah well I didn't catch all of that," Ben mumbled as he loosened up his tie, pulled it off and hung it on the hook that was connected to the inside of his closet door."

"Are you serious, you know the pastor doesn't miss anything that goes on in his church. If I didn't know any better I'd think you were losing your mind. Come on now you just witnessed them about to fight and their facial expressions don't make it any better." I said sitting on the edge of the bed wonder what Bentley was really thinking about.

"I guess that is a thing you women do but I guess he did bring a great message. I don't have time for all that nonsense. That's why I stay by myself that way I don't have to worry about nobody getting on my bad side." He replied as if this was a conversation he wanted no part of.

"You women! What is that supposed to mean Bentley? You make it seems as if we got something going on with each other. I have nothing to do with that and from the looks of it you got a part of it yourself. I don't know what has your pants in a bunch lately but I suggest you dig them out real soon if you don't want to see the old Glinda come out of me." I told him before hanging my church clothes on the back of my closet and walking out the room. I didn't want to choke the life out of him so I had to remove myself from his space to take a breath. I don't know how small talked turned into something so ugly.

Bentley

Glinda was upset with me because I guess you can say I made something out of nothing. I know Nakita is her friend but I feel like they are being too hard on Sharon. Glinda says that she isn't taking anyone's side but me knowing how she feels about Kita, I would bet money she was closer to Kita's side than Sharon's. I just don't have the energy for that type of drama in my life right now.

I got tired of dodging the church and thought that I would go and organize the coats for the sale we are having this weekend. I grabbed my jacket off the back of the sofa and went outside, jumped in my truck and headed down to the church. On my way, I stopped my Mc'Donald's and bought myself a medium Moca Frappe.' The taste hit my taste buds and melted in my mouth and I enjoyed every sip I took. Five minutes later I was driving into the parking lot of the church.

I got out of the truck and noticed Sharon's car was still parked out in front of the church. I guess Nova hadn't taken the time to come by and check on his wife's car. I was beginning to see why Sharon was feeling me now. She knows that I make sure that Glinda has any and everything she needs.

Preaching down at the church gives me enough to help Glinda with the bills and my bank account has a decent amount saved up from the job I had before we moved here. Not to mention the money I got when my parents got killed by an 18-wheeler a few years back. I was left with a lot of money from my lawsuit. The guy was texting and driving and wasn't paying attention to the road but I really don't want to revisit that thought.

Walking into the office the first person I saw was Sharon. I guess she had the same idea as me. She was hard at work going through boxes, pulling out coats and placing them on hangers. I detour before she saw me and went to see if Pastor Elton was in his office. Like always he was at his desk looking over papers. One thing I can say about him is he is going to make sure that every penny that comes into his church is on point and if anything is spent he will know what it was spent on.

"Good morning Pastor how are you this fine day?" I asked him and I knocked on his door before walking in sitting down in the chair in front of him.

Pulling the glasses, he had sitting on his noes down he looked up and said, "I am fine. How about yourself?" with a wide grin spread across his face.

"I could be better Pastor." I see you working hard in here this morning." I told him looking at him with a warm smile.

"Bentley tell me how have you and the Lord been doing?" He asked me jokingly but looking as he was waiting for a for real answer.

"Well, I think me and the Lord are getting along just fine," I replied.

"You think! You are a deacon man it isn't any time for thinking you got to know how a relationship with the Lord is. Boy if you were to ask me how was my relationship I would have told you. My relationship couldn't be better. I give the lord my heart and soul. Without him, I would be noting and you wouldn't be either." He told me and I couldn't do anything but put my head down in shame because he caught me slipping on that one.

"You're right pastor, you are so right. Look, I don't want to keep you from doing your work. I just came in to say hello. I am going to go help Sharon get ready for the sale we are having this weekend." I said to him as I stood up and pushed my chair up and left the room.

The pastor nodded his head as I walked out and made my way back to the office were Sharon was still as busy as a bee. I walked in and tapped her on the shoulder. She must have been in her own little world because when I did that it scared her. The coat flew one way and the hanger went the other.

"Ben, you scared the devil out of me. You better be careful coming in here like that you are going to catch one of these hangers around your little boney neck." She fussed walking over to giving me a hug. When she did that I didn't want to let go of her. That channel perfume she had on had my knees weak.

"Sharon, you are smelling really nice today girl," I told her causing her to smile the most beautiful smile I have ever seen in a while.

"Thank you! You aren't smelling bad yourself. What is that polo or something," she asked?

"No ma'am it isn't that's Nautica baby," I said as we both began to laugh because I said it like I had won an award for the man with the best smell.

I thought I better start picking up coats and place them on hangers with Sharon before we both started something and end up getting caught by Pastor Elton. We spent a few hours getting all the coats hung up. I found a few racks in the storage in the basement of the church to hang the coats on. Once we were all done Sharon and I stored all the coats down in the basement, to keep them out of the way of anyone that needs to come in and out of the church.

When we got them, all stored we said our goodbyes and headed out to the parking lot to leave. I noticed Sharon got in her car, started it up and drove off. I guess I was wrong Nova did take care of that problem. Then, on the other hand, knowing Sharon she may have taken something a loose to get me over to her house I just can't put anything past her. I shook my head and went on home to face my family.

When I got there Glinda was home and done with dinner. She was sitting on the couch watching the news. I walked in and spoke and she gave me a look that sent chills up my spine. I threw my keys on the kitchen counter and went to my room gather me some clean clothes and went to take a shower. I was all dusty from moving things around in the basement trying to find something to hang the coats on. I took my time so I could clear my mind. I know Glinda is mad but I don't see anything wrong with what I said about her and Nakita the other day. Oh well, I guess if she wants to be mad then that's on her. I will just stay out of her way until she ready to talk to me.

When I came out of the shower my wife and son had eaten dinner without me. I went to the kitchen and fixed my plate and sat down at the table alone. I started eating and my mouth became dry. I looked beside my plate and noticed I had forgotten to pour me a drink. I wanted to ask her if she would get me something but the look she gave me earlier made me think twice. I jumped up walked into the kitchen and grabbed a bottle of water out of the frig and popped the top before I could even sit back down at the table.

Once I was all done I went back to my room and stretched out on the bed and watched a good old western movie. Glinda was laying on the couch with Benny at the other ending watching whatever it is that they were watching. A few minutes later I got a text message from Sharon saying, "Hey Ben why don't you stop by my house before you go to the church tomorrow. I got an idea I been working on. I would like for you to look at it and tell me what you think of it." I smiled and sent her back a text letting her know I would be there before getting back into my movie.

A few hours later Glinda came walking into the room and went straight to the bathroom without cutting an eye at me. I have to admit it was killing me inside that she wasn't speaking to me but I didn't feel like I was in the wrong this go around. I just ignored her and got up to go ask Benny if he wanted to play a game of Taken on his PlayStation. When he jumped up running toward his room I knew I had just made his day. It is not often that the two of us play his game together but when we do it makes him super excited.

Benny and I got so into the game that we didn't realize that we had our outside voices going inside the house. I guess we were too loud for Glinda or she just was being ugly but she walked up and slammed the door so hard it scared both Benny and me." What's wrong with mama?" Benny asked with his hand across his chest like Fred Sandford when he was faking a heart attack.

"I don't know son but give me a minute daddy is going to find out," I told him as I got up and stormed out the room, shutting the door behind me so he couldn't hear our conversation.

I walked into the room and she was sitting on the couch with her feet curled up under her behind. "Can you tell me what made you so mad that you had to come and slam that door like that. You almost gave our son a heart attack. You really need to chill with your little attitude Glinda cause all this you got going on ain't that serious." I said trying to sound like I meant business.

"Look don't you come in here telling me how to react. You started this by putting me in the middle of someone's mess that I had nothing to do with. So, don't tell me what is not serious. Yes, Kita is my friend but I don't have anything against Sharon. I was trying to be neutral in the situation. Don't try me Ben because I will show you a side of me that I buried a long time ago. You better go play that game with Benny and try to keep down the noise. Y'all are not outside, that screaming echoes all over this house." She said that seems like in one sentence, and I knew if I wanted to keep my life I better move around. Besides I didn't want to argue in front of my son.

I walked back in the room and told Benny we had to keep it down a little bit. We played the game for a little longer before I made him clean-up for bed and I went to go get a little reading in out of the ole good book. I needed a word are two to help me get back in line with God. I feel like I have been straying and that may be what is causing our relationship to go bad. Once I was done I spent some time in my own zone talking to God. After spending time talking to Him I started to feel a little better about things.

The next morning, I got up a little early to try and smooth things over with Glinda but she was already gone. I peeked in Benny's room and he was putting his book bag on getting ready to go out and catch the bus. I went into the kitchen and grabbed his lunch off the counter and decided that I would take him to school instead of letting him ride the bus.

"Hey, little man how about I take you to school instead of riding the bus," I asked Benny as I walked up handing him his lunch.

"That would be nice Dad but I want to ride the bus with my friend Caleb since I don't see him much anymore other than church." He responded to me. I was a little hurt but I understood he was a kid and kids love to spend time with their friends.

I watched him from the front porch while he ran out to the end of the driveway to catch the bus. When the bus drove away I locked the house up and got in my truck and drove over to Sharon's house to check out this project she has been working on. I had a lot on my mind so I didn't have an appetite to eat anything. I bypass Mc Donald's this morning and drove straight to Sharon's house. Several minutes later I was pulling up in her front yard jamming my Kirk Franklin. I was in such a good mood I knew there was nothing that was going to mess up my day.

As I got out of my truck I could see Sharon standing in the door with a fluffy pink housecoat on. I saw the bus in the distance going down the street so she must have been waving goodbye to her daughter because the boy's bus came by just a little while ago. The bus has to pass by Sharon's house before getting to mine that's how I knew it had to be her daughter's bus.

"Good morning Bentley come on in. You timed that perfect I was just waving my daughter off for school." She told me as I felt a knot forming in my throat hoping this was not another one of her setups.

"Good morning Sharon," I replied as I walked up to the door giving her a hug.

"Well come on in and we can sit at the kitchen table and look over the notes I jotted down for you. Would you like a cup of coffee," she asked me?

"Sure, that would be great. I would like it black with two teaspoons of sugar if you don't mind please and thank you," I replied.

"No problem," she said and not even a minute later she was sitting my cup down on the table in front of me.

I must say she does come up with some great ideas to help the church. We spent a few hours discussing how Pastor Elton would really be proud if we could pull a nice program off like the one Sharon has in mind. Sharon jumped up to refill my cup of coffee as I was looking back over her notes once more. I was so pleased with the whole idea.

The problem came in when Sharon placed the cup of coffee back down on the table in front of me. I could feel a slight blow in my ear and she began to rub my shoulders in a way that made my eyes roll back in my head. The nibble I felt in my ear made me lose all my religion at that moment I clear the kitchen table causing the coffee to spill all over her wooden tile floor.

We were lost in the passion so deep we didn't hear the door open and the footsteps of Nova until they were staying up over the both of us. When Nova moved to the drawer to grab the biggest knife he could find. I made my way out the back door with Sharon's robe wrapped around my thin body. I was as scared as a stray cat soaking wet out in the thunderstorm.

As I could hear the arguing of Nova and Sharon I made my way to the side garage door and climbed into the back of Sharon's car. I didn't have time to gather my clothes or my keys so there was no way for me to leave. I pulled the latch on the top of the back seat and when it folded down I slid into her trunk.

Soon I heard sirens coming so I know the neighbors had to call to polices as loud as they were. All I could think about was Glinda leaving me for good when she found out and me being kicked out of another church if Nova didn't kill us both first. Before the sirens made it to the house I heard tires speeding off. I didn't know if Nova had killed Sharon and was on the run or what to think until I heard her calling my name.

"Bentley, where are you? Nova has left come out and hurry before he returns. Sharon called out to me as I hurried out of the trunk of her car and made my way into the house.

I grabbed my clothes off the floor and put them on so fast you would have thought I was a firefighter going to put out a fire. I reached into my pocket pulled out my keys and noticed my cell phone was missing. Before I could say a word, Sharon started to talk.

"Nova took your cell phone he said he was calling Glinda and everyone else at the church and tell them all about our affair. He tried to take your truck and leave but I fought him to keep him from getting your keys. Bentley the police are getting close I need you to leave now before they get here I will handle everything myself." Sharon responded pushing me out the door.

I jumped in my truck and speed away looking back in my rearview mirror watching the police make their way up to Sharon's house. I didn't know if I should go home or not. I didn't know if Nova had called Glinda and if so was she home waiting for me. I slowly approached the house and noticed that she wasn't home yet because the garage door was still down. Normally during the day if she is home she left it up until it starts to get late.

I pulled in the yard got out of my car and walked to the front door before I could unlock the door it came flying open and I started feeling blows to my head. All I could do was cover my face because I didn't know what was going on or who was pounding on me until I heard Glinda's voice asking me what did I think I was doing sleeping around with Sharon?

I didn't know my wife had hands like that. She always told me not to bring the old side of her out and now I don't know who to fear more Her or Nova. I could taste the blood in my mouth from my busted lip as I tried to stand straight up and walk on in the house. I was able to walk in and she started in on me again. This time I was able to jump back and grab her hands.

"Glinda stop let me explain what happens first." I tried to plead with her but she wasn't hearing anything I had to say. I didn't know this woman was as strong as she was. It took every bit of my strength to hold her hands so that she couldn't hit me anymore.

"There is nothing to explain I asked you not to lie to me and you just couldn't do that. I had a feeling something was going on with you and her but I just blew it off. I want you to get your stuff and when I get back from picking my son up from school, you better be gone." Glinda fussed as she grabbed her keys and walked out the door.

Glinda

I got off early today trying to come home and work things out with Bentley from a previous fight we had. To think he was going behind my back with Sharon. I got a good mind to drive over to her house and give her a piece of what I just gave Bentley. I was so mad I did just that but when I saw the police in the yard talking to Nova I decided to keep it moving if I wanted to keep my freedom. Besides I have a son I have to raise.

I drove over to the school and sat out front and waited thirty minutes for school to be released. This way Bentley had time to get his clothes out of the house that I already prepacked for him. I knew it would take a little time so once Benny made it to the car I took him to Cheddars to have a nice dinner just him and I.

"Where's dad mom why didn't he come with us. This is his favorite place to eat." He asked me as he bit into the chicken fried steak he had ordered.

"Dad won't be with us for a while Benny. He has to go away for a while. You will have other times to go out to eat with him now hush up and enjoy your meal." I told him trying to keep him from questioning me about his dad again.

After we were done eating I let Benny order some cake and ice cream to stall a little more before we went home. I text back and forth with Kita discussing what had just transpired. She told me she had another hour before she got off and she would pick up Trey for Benny to play with while the two of us have some girl talk.

I waited twenty more minutes and Benny was all done. I paid our tab left a tip and we left out to go home. When we got in the car Benny kept watching me like he wanted to ask me a question. I kept my eyes glued to the road and drove straight home. Going this way, we had to drive past Sharon's house and it took everything in me not to stop over there and tear her head off. I wanted to shave that mustache she had been trying hard to hide off her top lip.

This chick had me heated to the point that I just wanted to drive my car straight through her front door. Thank the Lord I got my son with me. The police saved her earlier and my son saved her this time but she better pray the Lord touch me before I see her again. I know they say to give it to the Lord and let him fight your battle but at this point, I feel like that hasn't worked for me yet. I think I can handle her better than anyone at this point.

When I made it home Bentley had gotten all of his things out and was long gone. I sent Benny to his room and called my girl Kita for some girl talk. She told me to pack up a few clothes and come stay with her for a few days so I could clear my head. I knew she really was trying to keep me from hunting down Sharon and tagging that behind. I thought it was a good idea so Benny and I packed up and drove over to her house.

I knocked on the door one good time before Kita was swinging it open and rushing us on in. "Kita are you sure your husband will be cool with us coming in to invade you guys' privacy?" I asked her as she helps take the bag that we had and handing them over to her son to take in the guest room.

"Glinda my husband is out of town for a week on a business trip. So you just get comfortable on the couch and I will go and get the both of us a glass of ice tea." Kita said and walked out of the room before I could say another word.

She has always been a true friend and no matter what she always told me how she felt even if it hurt my feeling even if I didn't want to hear it. That's what I like about her the most. At this point, she is the only person that can keep me from making Sharon my speed bump if I see her in the streets.

"Now tell me what's got you so upset? What has Bentley done now?" Kita asked me not knowing it was this serious.

Without even thinking twice I blurted out, "Nova caught him having sex with Sharon."

The tea that Kita had just sip went flying across the room so fast, I barely moved out the way in time before she wet me up with it. "He did what? Girl let's go beat that chick down right now" Kita said jumping off the couch grabbing a jar of Vaseline off of her bar.

"Wait now you are supposed to be calming me down friend and you trying to get both of us locked up. Then who going to take care of the boys?" I jumped up and stood in the front of the door so she couldn't leave.

She was walking the floor mad like it was her husband that Sharon was cheating with. "I knew I didn't like that woman and now that I think about it that day at the store did seem a little wired," she blurted out.

"What do you mean by that Lakita?" I asked her standing in front of her waiting for her to spill the beans.

"The two of them were having some kind of disagreement when I walked upon them. I asked them was everything alright and she began to get a little defensive with me. I didn't think much about it after she made me upset and I wanted to slide her ratchet behind across the store." She replied and stood there looking as if she was staring into space.

"Oh really and you know when I questioned him about it that bum called himself accusing the two of us of picking on her," I told Kita and I could tell it almost sent her flying over the edge.

"So he did huh? That old string bean looking....." She was about to say before the boys entered the room.

"Benny is there something you need?" I asked him as he stood there looking at me like he knew something was going on.

"Mom is everything ok? You looked like something is bothering you.

"I tried to warn him about walking in on grownups when they are talking but he wouldn't listen to me. I told him you were with my mom Mrs. Glinda and that you were fine. He told me he knew when something was bothering you and he had to check on you."

"Benny baby I am fine. Kita and I are just having girl talk." I told him.

"Well if everything is alright why is Mrs. Kita standing there putting all that grease on her face and hands?" He asked me and when I turned around I could have passed out.

"Baby Mrs. Kita was a little ashy that's all. You two go back to the room and leave us to talk."

As they walked out of the living room I heard Trey whisper "Grownups can do some wired stuff sometimes."

"Benny chuckled and said, "Did she have to use the whole jar? How ashy was she?"

When they were gone I couldn't look Kita in her eyes for laughing so hard. "Dang Kita, I am like Benny did you use the whole jar?"

I knew that would make you laugh." Kita said using the towel on the back of the sofa to clean all of that darn grease off of her plump round face.

"Honey that was a laugh I needed. You were standing there looking like a chunky grease monkey. When that baby said, "did she have to use the whole jar?" "I could have died and come back when I saw your face. Nakita, girl you do the most." I told her laughing so hard I could barely catch my breath.

"Grease monkey, Glinda don't do me, girl. You know I was looking like a plump, juicy, glossy apple standing here," she replied trying hard not to laugh at the lie she just told.

"Look, Kita, I am tired I am about to go to bed. I can't keep playing around with you all night." I told her as I sit there and yawed over and over.

"Okay Glinda but before you go to bed. Tell me, what are you going to do about your situation with Ben.?"

"Nakita, I am done this time. He did this to me once and now again. There will not be a third time. I plan to continue to go to the church but as for me and him we are getting a divorce."

"Wow! Well, whatever you decide to do I am behind you. I would have probably let the devil use me and took his life after the first time he cheated but I am glad you did it God's way," Kita s said joking once again.

"You know what Kita I am going to bed on that note. See you in the morning I told her as I got up and walked to the room in which I would be sleeping.

It was nice being with Kita for a few days but it felt even better to be home again. I had time to clear my head and yes I still feel the pain from what Ben did to me by cheating with Sharon. That only lets me know that what they say about once a dog always a dog has some truth to it.

I really didn't feel like going to church this morning but I had to realize it wasn't God that cheated on me it was a man. I gave in and got dressed and Benny and I headed out the door and drove over to the church. What got me was the fact that Benny never once asked me where his dad was this morning. I believe he could tell that something was wrong but since he didn't ask I didn't volunteer to tell him either. Not because I didn't want to but because I wasn't ready to go into that with him right now.

Once Benny and I made it to the church we got out to walk in. The first thing I noticed was Bentley's truck parked under a big oak tree to the left of the parking lot. I started to feel weak in my stomach since it's been a week that we saw or talk to one another. I walked in and saw him sitting in the pulpit like he was a saint and started to get angry at the sight of his bony little face.

I went on in and found a seat next to Kita who was already sitting down and enjoying the song the choir was singing. I tapped her hand and pretended I didn't see Ben and started enjoying the song myself. I kept feeling like someone was watching me and I looked to the far right side of the choir stand and noticed Sharon trifling behind looking at me like I was out of line for coming to church. I gave her a dirty look before I looked down and began to pray. Lord knows if I was going to keep it together I had to pray and pray real hard.

After the singing was over and before the pastor got up to speak, Mrs. Brooks took all the kids out of the church. This was something that was odd because the children always stay and have service with us. I paid it no mind and just sat back to see what was next. When Bentley approached the stand instead of the pastor I grabbed Kita's hand so hard she let out a little sound and everyone looked back.

"I am so sorry, I just got so upset when I saw who was stepping up to bring the word today," I whispered to Kita while she was still rubbing her hand.

"Honey that hurt, I would hate for you to put hands on either of them," she whispered back to me.

Bentley was about to speak but before he could get a word out Sharon came and stood beside him and I could feel my blood boiling and my blood pressure shooting through the roof. I moved to get up to walk out but Kita pulled me back down. Tears were forming in my eyes I was so mad but I fought them back to see what this mess was all about.

"Good morning everybody. I know you all are used to the pastor speaking first on Sunday mornings but I asked him if I could stand first to confess something to the church today."

I couldn't believe this man had the nerves to get up and do this in front of the whole church. I felt knots balling up in my stomach but I didn't move I just sat there and listened.

I have been a deacon her for some time now and I have formed a tight bond with a lot of you here. I got so close that I was able to gain trust from each and every one of you. You trusted me with helping the pastor lead your souls to God. I hate to say that I have let you all down. I am helping you to do God's will and I haven't been acting accordingly myself. I see you all looking around like deacon what does that mean?"

I will tell you what I mean. Sharon and I have been working closely helping the pastor with different events down at the church to raise money. Well, one thing led to another and we let the devil in and things went a little too far. This led us to have an affair on our spouses. We not only betrayed you we hurt the people we loved the most and that were our families.

I come before you today to apologize not only to you but to my wife and son. I never meant to hurt any of you and if that means losing my position as being your deacon here I understand," he said right before he sat down.

I rolled my eyes thinking to myself this man can get one over on the church but him and I are done. I already started printing out my divorce paperwork and by next week after I have my attorney look at them I will be delivering them to him.

After Ben sat down Pastor Elton stood up and started to speak. "Ben has come to me and confessed his sins to me. I forgive him because God has forgiven me for many sins I once committed. Now if there is someone that doesn't feel comfortable with what Deacon Bentley has said today you are welcome to fellowship wherever you choose to. Just remember you too are not perfect and have sinned and fallen short of the glory many times. My question is did you want God to forgive you? Seems mighty quiet in here." He said standing there waiting for some members to get up and walk out.

Everyone just sits back and looked at Bentley like he did nothing wrong. I had to admit the pastor was right because I did some things back in the days I know I wasn't proud of. One thing I do know is I will forgive Ben but I will never forget. This is why I have to let him go. As long as we are together the trust will never be the same and if there is no trust then our relationship will never work.

Church was over and I grabbed Benny and left quickly because I couldn't see myself holding a conversation with Bentley. When we made it home I ordered a pizza and a 2-liter bottle of Pepsi. Once we were done eating I spent the rest of the day doing household chores while Benny did whatever in his room.

Seven long months later Bentley and I were legally divorced and he moved into a two bedroom apartment on the other side of two. That way when Benny wanted to come over he could feel like he was at home. He continued to work at the church but he also started a part-time job working at a small car lot as a car salesman. He agrees to pay me child support on his own to help Benny with things he may need. So far things have been going to plan. Since Sharon stopped working down at the church, he hasn't had to be around her and I guess that was a good thing for the both of them.

A few years have passed since Bentley and I have been divorced. Benny has been doing fine with spending the weekends and holidays with his dad. We agreed to co-parent with Benny as much as we could so that he would be able to still spend as much time with his dad just as much as he does with me. Bentley is in counseling now trying to help him with his womanizing habits.

I, on the other hand, have met a nice guy by the name of Jacoby Bryant. Jacoby just happened to be one of the officers from College Station Police Department that came out to Sharon and Nova's house the day she and Ben were caught red-handed by Nova. So he knew the story about my cheating ex-husband oh so well.

He is a very handsome, respectful oh and did I mention Christian man. He looks just like Lance Gross from the show "House of Pain" He is every bit of six-foot-one and his skin is like milk chocolate. This man has made me feel like a little high school girl all over again. Benny gets along with him so well. I tell you he is like a dream come true.

Bentley has even met him and is fine with him being around our son. He realizes what we had is over and just wants Benny and I to be happy. We all still attend the church and the members there all forgave Bentley and Sharon for their affair. Nova and Sharon worked out their differences and decided to stay together for their family. Kita is still the same crazy Kita. She does not trust the ground Sharon walks on and stay as far from her as she can. Who would have thought out of all the hell I been through in my life, things would turn out so much better for me? I now believe the saying when one door closes God will open another one. All I can say is Thank you God for my open door.

The End

Dedication

I want to dedicate this book to my late father Bishop G.H. Jones III. He has been my biggest supporter for forty long years. Anything I set out to do he has always cheered me on. He let me know that anything is possible as long as I have faith and believe in God. This man has been my hero all of my life. I know they say no one is perfect but he was more than perfect in my eyes. He was a true man of God and always lived his life to please God. He taught my sibling's and me right from wrong from children and continued into our adulthood. One of his mottos was its God's way or no way and with him, it was always about God. October 5, 2017, was the day he gained his wings and took a big piece of my heart with him. I will forever miss his wise advice and his anointed prayers. When that man prayed I know for sure God received that message faster than a 911 call. While on his deathbed he hardly had the energy to speak but when visitors came to visit and pray for him, he ended the visit with a powerful prayer of his own. That is what you call a true soldier in the army of the lord. R.I.H Dad, I will forever keep you in my heart. I will never say goodbye but see you later when God calls me home.

November 11, 1948 to October 05, 2017

Made in the USA
Coppell, TX
02 February 2020

15319723R00072